Peter Szondy

A former documentary and commercial filmmaker, Peter Szondy is an internationally published poet, educated at the University of Vienna and Loyola Marymount University. He lives in Ojai, CA.

Based On A Story By:

G. M. Mercier

G.M. ("Mike") Mercier was steeped in spiritual activism from early childhood. His mother was a prominent church administrator. Mike is a prolific and successful screenwriter and has helped fund over forty independent films. He lives in Lake Elsinore, CA.

The Mustard Seed

A Novel

By

Peter Szondy

Based on a Story by

G. M. Mercier

Printed in the United States of America.

Library of Congress Cataloging in Publication Data
is available upon request.

ISBN 978-0-9971369-2-0: Soft Cover Edition
ISBN 978-0-9971369-3-7: Hard Cover Edition

Learn more about "The Mustard Seed" and connect with your Christian Community to share your miracles, hear about other Christian miracles and tell your fellow Christians how you found the love of Jesus Christ.

To do this visit us at http://www.themustardseedbook.com

Cover design by Jane Gerling

TRAILMAKER PRODUCTIONS, LLC
1310 Venice Blvd., Suite 200
Venice, CA 90291
www.TrailmakerProductions.com
info@themustardseedbook.com

To Janie,

The Love Of My Life,

Always, Peter

Truly I tell you, anyone who will not receive the kingdom of God like a little child will never enter it.

Luke 18:17

He presented another parable to them, saying,

"The kingdom of heaven is like a mustard seed, which a man took and sowed in his field; and this is smaller than all other seeds, but when it is full grown, it is larger than the garden plants and becomes a tree, so that the birds of the air come and nest in its branches."

The Mustard Seed

Preface

While this novel is clearly a work of fiction, the underlying inspiration for it is not. Years ago, my family and I endured a trauma that left my outlook on just about everything fundamentally altered. My eight-year-old granddaughter had been diagnosed with a tumor so closely melded to her heart that it was nearly inoperable and was virtually untreatable. With the outlook grim at best, we all began to pray very much in earnest. It was the events that followed which inspired me to write the story of THE MUSTARD SEED in the form of a screenplay. It is the same inspiration that animates this novel, which my friend and collaborative partner Peter Szondy has written. He has captured the heart-felt quality that led me to write the original story. I find it truly inspiring and I hope you do as well.

-- G. M. Mercier

CHAPTER 1

There was a time not long ago that Sam Donovan didn't believe in God. The few people in the valley who thought they really knew him would have guessed Sam probably had some sort of faith, if for no other reason than he'd survived too many firefights not to know somebody had been looking out for him. Beyond that, he was the first to admit that something always used to hold him back from doing a whole lot of praying. It wasn't really that he didn't believe. The way Sam saw it, God bailing him out of trouble in Vietnam was one thing. After all, he was Special Forces, defending his country. That kind of providence he could accept. Seemed a sensible thing for God to do. But for all that, he felt it would be presumptuous to think of that courtesy as a personal invitation to, say, take up space in a pew in God's congregation. No, that he never quite felt up to.

It's not that he didn't have opportunity. His beloved wife, Rachel, was very devout. When she was alive, she took their daughter, Bonnie, to church most Sundays. And Sam could always hear the church bells of White Dove. He wasn't actually in church, of course, nor even nearby, but the sound carried from down in the village on the wind, however faintly, up the valley and high into the hills, as he walked the trail near his horse ranch, where he'd grown up. No, Sam knew perfectly well where the Sunday services were. But after coming back from the wars in Vietnam and Nicaragua to his old home near some of the wilder hills of Southern California, he formed some solitary habits; got used to keeping pretty much to himself, preferring his own observances.

On Sundays, in the half-light before dawn, Sam would hang a plaid, red flannel Pendleton on his broad-shouldered six-foot-four frame and tuck his Levi's into his boots. Then he would set off hiking, along with Butch, his black Labrador, who was like Sam in many ways: old and tough, but still not bad looking and liked to have his belly rubbed. Though in his sixties, Sam was still lean and strong, Green Beret vet that he was. His daughter, Bonnie, had always told him he looked like Clint Eastwood, with his sandy gray hair and steely blue eyes. On the one hand he allowed how he thought that was a load of hooey, but he had to admit it made him smile. Of course, most things Bonnie did made him smile. Together he and Butch would go up the narrow trail by the creek that ran along the paddock at the back of his property. From there they walked further up to the foot of the mountain, where he could see the sunrise cast a pale glow of pink on the cliffs above. At trail's end they would arrive at the most beautiful place in the world – White Dove Lake – where the two of them could sit on the shore and watch the new day unfold as the golden light raked across the glass of the wooded lake, framed by cedars and pines. He would savor the moments of this timeless blessing of woodland and water. The Chumash, who had lived here for ten thousand years before the Spanish arrived, called this place the Lake of the Sky Spirits. Sam would enjoy the silence and the stillness, along with the mallards and geese and wood ducks and white-tailed deer and jack-rabbits.

For many years, these walks to the lake were as close as Sam got to any praying. He felt like in his days he had taken and survived about every stone life could throw. He had looked down a lot of different kinds of gun barrels pointed his way and somehow, when the dust settled, he would always end up as the one who went walking away; he just knew he was that guy. He trusted himself in that way. And it had always worked. Alright, not entirely, but generally, it worked well enough. Until something happened that made it all stop working. Totally. And everything changed.

CHAPTER 2

It all began one Sunday in early Spring, when there was still a little snow on the mountaintops, the same day that Sam rescued Steve Cleary's pale ale. The same day that Sam's grand-daughter first saw Jesus. And Sam, who thought he had made peace with his demons and finally had his life under control, suddenly found himself faced with losing what he loved most in this life. He had faced down so many fears before. But this one left him feeling blind and hopeless. He was shaken to the core and his whole world changed in a way that no one could have imagined, least of all Sam Donovan.

Upon that Sunday morning down in the village of White Dove, the parking lot of the one-hundred-year-old little white clapboard church that housed The Congregation of White Dove was full of trucks, vans, station wagons and sedans. A few of them were new vehicles, but mostly not. A beautiful soprano voice could be heard from inside the church, singing "Amazing Grace." Sam, as usual, had come down from the mountain and drove his '97 silver Dodge pick-up right past the church. He parked down the street in front of Maria's Cantina Mazatlan, which was about as close to a "hang out" in the village as Sam had. There he went in and sat at the bar and quietly ate his huevos rancheros. This was a charming, intimate place with rustic Mexican pigskin-covered cedar-strip chairs and a salsa bar with selections ranging from melt-your-brain-hot habanero and chipotle, all the way down to white-bread, gringo strength pico de gallo. Sam favored the hotter sauces and mostly he showed up there because of Maria herself. Maria de la Paz, a beautiful Latina in her early forties with flashing eyes, for her part, had to admit she more than noticed this big laconic hunk of a guy who seemed to show up and sit at her bar like clockwork every Sunday.

Meanwhile, in the church a few doors down, Sam's thirty-one-year-old daughter, Bonnie, and her husband, Alex Hopkins, joined with the congregation in the chorus of "Amazing Grace." One of the sweetest voices in the church belonged to their tow-headed eight-year-old daughter, Sara. The hymns seemed to come naturally to her. Their ten-year-old son, Danny, was also there, if slightly less voluntarily. The Hopkins' were a beautiful family and most people in town thought of them that way. Not so much because of Alex; he was a regular-looking mug, but strong and kind. It was Bonnie who lit up the stars in any room she walked into, all without losing her level head. She was a drop-dead gorgeous strawberry blonde, but in a down-to-earth way, and there was a thoughtfulness about her that came naturally. She seemed to make people around her feel happy. And little Sara was Bonnie in miniature. Sweet by nature and precociously smart, as well as looking adorable, with clear eyes as wide and as blue as the sky above White Dove Lake.

Meanwhile, as Sam poured extra-picante salsa on his eggs, Maria stood behind her bar and smiled at Sam. "No church this morning?" she asked.

He smiled at her, shrugged and said, "Well,... it's not something I usually do. Not sure why. How come you're not at mass?"

"I went last night. Today I have to work," she said. "I've got a sick daughter at home."

"Ah." He could see that she looked worried. "How's your daughter doing?"

She shook her head. "Not good. How are your grandchildren?"

Sam had been eating at Maria's Cantina off and on for a couple of years. He felt naturally drawn to her and there was something about him that she clearly liked. But Sam was one widower who was not to be moved easily. Some part of him feared disappointing Maria. Maybe even scaring her. Underneath it all, he was careful of giving his heart. He had been so happy with Rachel and was so broken when she died, that the thought of opening himself up to anything like that again was something he hadn't yet felt ready for.

"They're both doing good," Sam said of his grandchildren. "Someday it might be nice if you and your daughter could meet them."

"I would love that," said Maria, "but she's not well and it's hard for her to get out of bed. I don't think we'll be able to."

Sam nodded. "I understand."

And Sam did understand. And he felt a little guilty. It made him grateful for the health of his own family, who at that moment were listening to the genial Pastor Bob Jenkins, Jr., holding forth on the text for the day, Matthew 17, verse 20:

"So when the disciples asked Jesus how come they couldn't drive out the demon themselves, he replied, 'Because you have so little faith. Truly I tell you, if you have faith as small as a mustard seed, you can say to this mountain, "Move from here to there," and it will move. Nothing will be impossible for you.'"

Little Sara listened raptly and drank in every syllable like water. It all made sense to her. Her brother, Danny, was... well, he was intent, too, but more about looking forward to going home and playing Nintendo.

Bonnie listened to the sermon with one ear but mostly she just smiled at her kids. And Alex was just happy that Bonnie was comfortable.

Maria was not eager to talk more about her sick daughter and went about wiping off the bar and bussing dishes. Then as Sam was nearly finished with his plate, they heard suddenly voices raised at a nearby table: "Hey, that's my beer you're drinking!"

That was Steve Cleary, who owned the best used-book shop in town, sitting with his little cousin, Ernie, and trying to have a beer with his brunch. Nick Carter had other ideas as he grabbed Steve's bottle, stood there and guzzled it down in one shot. Nick and his brother, Ryan, were tall and rough in a biker style and almost as tough as they looked, standing over the diminutive, nerdy-looking Steve. When Nick was done, he belched and slapped the empty down on the table. What the Carter boys were a little too drunk pick up on was that Sam had known them since their childhood, although their paths hadn't crossed in a few years, as Sam had served in Vietnam with their daddy.

"Okay, I need you both to leave if you can't behave yourselves," said Maria. She reached under the bar, grabbed another bottle of Sierra Nevada Pale Ale and opened it: "Here, Steve, I'm sorry."

Ryan just grinned at Nick then stepped over and started to grab the beer Maria had just opened, but Sam, without looking up, reached over and grabbed Ryan's arm.

"I don't think that's a good idea," said Sam.

"Take your hand off me while you still have one," said Ryan.

"As soon as you let go of Steve's beer."

"Or what, Old Man?" said Ryan with a sneer. "Do you know who you're talking to? I could hurt you real bad."

Meanwhile, the final notes of another chorus of "Amazing Grace" drifted into the street and the church doors swung open. The worshippers who came pouring out were a cross-section of the town: folks of all ages and cultures and walks of life, but mostly families -- young children, teenagers and their parents. Along with the Hopkins', there came the Millers, Walter and Flora, and their sandy-haired, grade-school-age brood, Ellen, Sylvia and Mark; although Mark wasn't really walking; he was in the motorized wheelchair that had been his legs since the car accident two years ago. Then came Doctor David Riley, African-American, age fifty-seven, the local M.D., who helped

The Mustard Seed

his slightly portly wife, Elizabeth, down the steps.

As Sara walked across the church parking lot next to Mark in his wheelchair, Mark focused on two high-school boys playing basketball across the street. One of them put away a good-looking slam-dunk.

"I wish I had a picture of me doing that," said Mark. "I would hang it on my bedroom wall."

"Could you do that before the accident?" asked Sara. She had always liked Mark.

"Sure."

"Really?"

"Yeah, when my father lifted me up to the hoop, I could do it no problem."

Sara laughed. "My parents are coming. I have to go. I'll see you in school tomorrow. Come on, Danny, we've got to go."

"Okay, I'm coming," said Danny, trying to tear himself away from chatting up the cute nine-year-old, Sylvia Miller, while he reflexively combed his hair. Danny may not have been practically perfect like Sara, but he was a good kid, too. And yes, he also got his mother's good looks. But he was, after all, "a guy" and it was an aspiration he worked hard at. The important thing was to be cool. Or no, actually the most important thing was to look cool. So when Danny emerged from church, he had pulled out the comb from his back pocket and made sure his little wave was just so. He sure liked that little wave. Sara, from her arched expression toward Danny, seemed less than impressed.

Alex and Bonnie noticed Sarah's eye-rolling look, but then as the parents shared a knowing glance, Alex shrugged and said quietly to Bonnie, "Hey, little sisters always think they're wiser than their brothers, no matter what the age. All my sisters keep giving me advice. And I'm forty next month."

Fortunately for Danny, he didn't care about Sara's opinions, mainly because he was oblivious to them. She was his sister whom he loved and would defend to the death, but her opinions weren't supposed to make sense. Because she was his sister. And he was a guy. And he was cool. And he had great hair.

Bonnie looked on at her family and just smiled. They made her happy.

And, oh yes, as Ryan was clutching Steve Cleary's bottle of Sierra Nevada Pale Ale and Sam was holding Ryan's wrist in the vise of his grip, Sam just smiled at him.

"And all this time," said Sam. "I was thinking what a sweet little boy you used to be. Shows you what I know."

Ryan threw a right cross at Sam, who, in one seamless motion, stepped off his stool, blocked the punch and hit Ryan in the throat with an open hand. Ryan grabbed his throat. His knees buckled and Sam was suddenly behind him, slamming Ryan's forehead into the bar, knocking him half unconscious. Sam turned to find himself facing Nick, who took a karate stance.

Sam shook his head and smiled. Nick did a step punch at Sam's face. Sam blocked and dropped under the punch, then foot-swept Nick's foot out from under him. As Nick hit the ground, Sam fell to one knee onto Nick's solar plexus and knocked the wind out of him, leaving him doubled up. Ryan was still clutching his throat trying to breathe.

"Nick and Ryan Carter," said Sam, shaking his head as he pulled their wallets from their back pockets. "I know it feels like you're going to die, but you won't." He pulled the drivers licenses from their wallets. "Just relax and you'll catch your breath in a minute or two."

Sam tossed them back their wallets as he looked at their ID's. "No, you won't die today. Unless of course your father finds out about this. Yeah, I've known your daddy, Chuck, since he was a little kid. Know him well. We were in Special Forces together in Vietnam. A good man, your daddy."

Nick and Ryan, still mute from wheezing, shared a look of panic.

"But," Sam continued, "I don't think this is something he needs to find out about, do you? So I'll tell you what." Sam tossed their licenses back to them. "I'll buy you both a beer and we'll keep this between us. If you promise to behave."

The brothers nodded. Sam turned to Maria, pulled some bills out of his pocket and laid them on the bar. "Why don't you get these boys a couple of beers. I have to get home. Got me some wood to chop."

As the church finally emptied out, Pastor Bob Jenkins, Jr., and his wife, Lucy, stood in the doorway, shaking many hands and bidding all a safe road home. As they watched their flock get into cars and drive away, the gray-haired couple appeared for all the world like parents looking wistfully after their children after they had stopped by for a short visit. And in truth that's exactly how Pastor Jenkins thought of all his congregants -- as his children. In fact, the Pastor and his wife behaved that way with pretty much everyone, with near-parental care, whether they showed up at their services or not. Many's the meal that local needy people picked up from Lucy at the back door of the rectory, and the Jenkins' were always active in many local social aid organizations. That's the way it had always been, a labor of love, dating from the days in the late 1950's when Pastor Bob's father, the late Pastor Bob, Sr., founded the Congregation of White Dove Church.

Still, even though the Jenkins tried to love everyone equally, they did enjoy some of them more than others. And none more than the Hopkins Family. But then, everyone loved the Hopkins Family. How could they not?

As Bonnie and her family pulled up in the blue Ford Explorer to their three-bedroom house with the manicured green lawn and the two bicycles in the front yard and the red Ford pick-up in the driveway, Bonnie set the day's agenda for the kids:

"If you are going to go see your Grandpa, you need to change your clothes and if you want to take your bikes, put them in the back of the car."

Sara looked at Danny. "I'll race you," she said.

"Okay." Danny ran for the house with Sara right on his heels.

Alex yelled after them, "Both of you slow down!" The kids slammed the front door. Alex frowned.

Bonnie just smiled. "They'll be fine, Alex."

"I know," said Alex.

"Coming to my Dad's with me?"

"You go," he said. "I need to finish the patio deck today."

Meanwhile, Danny, in his room, frantically pulled up his pants, grabbed his shirt, stopped, looked in the mirror and laid his shirt on the dresser. He combed his hair and admired himself in the mirror. Then he put the comb back in his pocket. This was all very important stuff. Then Danny came flying out of his bedroom, putting on a T-shirt as he ran past Alex who was opening a bottle of orange juice in the kitchen.

"Slow down!" Alex yelled.

Danny stopped when he realized the T-shirt over his head had messed up his hair. He pulled out the comb and, yep, combed his hair.

"Did Sara come out of her room yet?" Danny asked.

"She's outside," said Alex.

"Oh no," said Danny; he put away the comb and ran outside, where Sara was already putting her bike in the back of the SUV.

"That's not fair," said Danny, sulking as he grabbed his bike. Sara started to help him load it in the back.

"How did you get out here so quick?" he asked.

"I didn't take time to comb my hair," she laughed and ran her fingers through his hair.

"Don't touch the hair," said Danny, "I just combed it! Never, ever touch the hair!"

Sara loved to mess with Danny's hair; she thought he was so cute and funny when he flipped out about it. But she knew when to stop. Besides, she was looking forward to two of her favorite things: seeing her Grandpa and riding down to the lake.

CHAPTER 3

The road to Grandpa's ranch took Bonnie and her kids just a few miles up the state highway into the hills, to Upper White Dove, an area where bears and mountain lions were frequent visitors and condors felt at home. Bonnie, too, felt at home here. The ranch, along with the valley and the town of White Dove, was the nest she had grown up in. Her family started ranching here in the 1870's and now, as she drove with her brood back to the old homestead, through orange and avocado groves and horse ranches and vineyards, she smiled to herself at how comfortable and happy she had become with her old home, which now as she and Alex raised their children here, seemed ever new.

The weathered old signage at the stone gate on the highway said, "El Rancho de la Paloma Blanca" -- The Ranch of the White Dove. Bonnie smiled and turned into the private road that was Sam's long driveway. After a minute's drive, she pulled up the Explorer to a 1906 craftsman-style ranch house, surrounded by a grove of gnarly coast live oaks and sycamores.

Sara and Danny jumped out of the car immediately. "Let's go down to the lake!" said Sara. "No, I don't want to," said Danny. "Grandpa said I could play Nintendo."

"No, please, it's too beautiful to be inside," Sara said. "You can fish."

Danny gave this some thought, then replied, "Okay, but what are you going to do?"

"I just like being there," said Sara, "but I'll bring a fishing pole, and maybe I'll fish, too."

Danny gave a quick glance to their mother who now stood behind them. Bonnie just smiled and shrugged her okay.

"Alright, but let's eat first" said Danny. "I'm hungry."

Sara answered, "No, let's pack a lunch and we'll have a little picnic. I'll race you there on the bike."

"That wouldn't be fair. I'm bigger than you," said Danny."

"It's okay if you win," Sara said.

Danny just shook his head and smiled at her. "You're too nice, Sara. It's not normal."

It was then that Grandpa's dog, Butch, the old black Labrador, ran up to Sara and gave her a reunion face-licking, along with a dance of unbounded tail-wagging and leaping, ecstatic joy that only a dog could pull off. To Butch, Sara was a puppy he had helped to raise and he always treated her like the family she was.

"We'll take Butch with us," said Sara, suddenly inspired.

"Okay. But maybe we shouldn't race."

Sara smiled, "Okay."

Danny looked at her and thought about it for a moment. On the other hand, he does love to win and he's older and stronger... so... why not?

"No, let's race," said Danny.

Sara was about to shrug in agreement just as Sam Donovan walked out onto the front porch and looked at his two grandchildren. "You two aren't planning on stealing my dog are you?"

"Just for the day, Grandpa," said Sara. "We're going to ride down to the lake."

Sam smiled. "Well, you could always keep him if you're willing to feed him."

Sara looked over at Butch, like she was half considering it.

"He eats too much. We couldn't afford it," she said.

"Always knew you were smarter than me," said Sam.

The two kids ran over and gave their Grandpa a hug. Sam was just as enthralled by his grandkids as Butch was, even if he couldn't show it with as much tail wagging. As Bonnie watched with pleasure and walked by them on her way to the house, she said, "I guess I should pack you both a lunch?"

The Mustard Seed

"Okay," answered Sara.

"Say grace before you eat."

"We will, Mom," said Sara.

Danny raced seriously through the woods, putting all his strength into the pedals. Sara not so much. She carried the two fishing poles, enjoyed the ride and was content to come in second. Butch loped along behind her. She loved everything about the lake. The beauty of the approach up the bike path through the woods was topped only by the lake itself, the shimmering reflections of the trees and the mountain in the water and the way the light changed as the sun moved across the sky and cast the entire scene in new and varied shades and colors by the hour.

"I won!" said Danny as he dropped his bike and looked back at Sara.

"I know. You went really, really fast," she said, smiling at him.

"I did, didn't I?"

"You sure did."

Meanwhile, Sara noticed that Butch had wandered over by a tree and was sniffing at something. She put the fishing poles on the ground and on taking a closer look, she found Butch sniffing around a dead bird.

"Stop it, Butch," she said. "Danny, call Butch over to you."

"Butch, come here."

But Butch wasn't going anywhere, so she had to push him away so she could pick up the bird.

Danny cringed a little. "What are you doing?" he asked.

"It's a bird," she said, staring intently at it as she held it softly. "I think it's a sparrow."

"Yeah, I know that, but it's dead. And it's kind of gross. Shouldn't you put it down and like maybe bury it?"

"No, it might not be dead."

Danny peers at the bird's chest. "Its heart isn't beating. It's not breathing. That's dead."

Sara keeps studying the bird. "Maybe if we pray, he'll come back to life."

"Sara, he's dead," said Danny. "Nothing can bring him back."

"Lazarus was dead for four days and Jesus brought him back."

Now Danny started to get almost indignant. "Sara, trust me, the bird isn't Lazarus and Jesus isn't here."

"Yes, he is," said Sara. "Jesus is always with us."

"I don't see him," said Danny.

"He's still here."

"But he hasn't brought anyone back to life in two thousand years."

"We don't know that," said Sara, "and God can do anything."

"But you're not God," said Danny, "and the bird is dead."

"Okay," said Sara, "but Jesus told us that we can do the same things he did – if we believed in him."

"He did?" said Danny. "You're making this up, right?"

"No, I'm not, he really said that! And do you remember what Jesus said about the mustard seed?"

"No," said Danny, "I can't say that I do."

"We were just at church today, Danny, and the Pastor was talking about it."

Danny just shrugged. Sara smiled at her brother. "Jesus said if we had faith even as small as a mustard seed, we could move a mountain."

Danny thought about that. He looked up at the mountain, took a deep breath, took out his comb and dragged it carefully through his hair. "I think you'll have as much luck moving that mountain as you do bringing back the bird. It's just not going to happen."

"It might," said Sara.

"Really?"

"Maybe. I mean, I love birds," said Sara.

Danny looked at the smile on Sara's face. "You love everyone and everything." He couldn't keep from smiling back at her. Who could? Besides, he knew he wouldn't win any arguments with his sister; hadn't happened yet and if he did what would be the point? "Okay," he threw up his hands. "Bring the bird back to life."

Sara reached out and brushed her free hand against Danny's arm. She was grateful for even such a tiny blessing from her brother, even if given half-heartedly and with a dose of whimsy. Then with the bird in her hand, she walked slowly, almost solemnly to the shore of the lake where she carefully knelt down on the sand and began to pray the Lord's Prayer aloud: "Our Father, which art in heaven, hallowed be thy name. Thy kingdom come, thy will be done on earth as it is in heaven."

Danny sat bemused on a log at the edge of the woods as he watched his sister go off into what seemed some kind of trance by the lakeshore.

Sara continued to pray: "Give us this day our daily bread..." and after a while -- Danny wasn't sure how long -- but a long enough time to get him a little antsy, Butch came and sat next to Danny and looked up at him, as if to say, "Well, are you going to play with me, or what?" It became clear to Danny and Butch that Sara wasn't going to join them anytime soon, so Danny picked up a stick and began to play fetch with the old dog. Butch was grateful.

"I'm going to go play with Butch in the woods," Danny shouted to Sara. If she heard him she gave no sign. Her voice had grown silent now but her lips kept moving as she stared out at the lake, seemingly in some place of her own.

After an hour of fetch in the woods, Butch got bored; the stick seemed to lose its attraction. So Danny decided to do some fishing. He picked up his pole and chose a spot a little ways down the shore from where Sara still prayed. That way he could stay out of her way but still watch over her from the corner of his eye. Sara was still on her knees, still in her special thrall, unchanged.

Hours had now passed. Danny by now had pulled four rainbow trout from the lake and could feel his patience draining. He had half-finished one of the sandwiches Bonnie had packed for them and as the sky grew more orange and pink, he saw the sun descend toward a distant mountain peak. Sara still prayed, now not even moving her lips, just gazing into the mist that formed over the far side of the lake. Danny took it on himself to approach her. As he got closer, he saw the dead bird still in her hands.

"Sara, we should go," Danny said quietly. "If you want I'll help you bury it."

Sara reacted not a whit, just stared out across the lake.

Danny's brow furrowed and he spoke now in a serious tone. "Sara, it's getting late and it might rain. We should go home."

Nothing.

"Okay," said Danny, "we'll stay a little longer but it's going to get cold out here and if it starts to rain, we'll be soaking wet by the time we get home and we'll get in trouble. Mom's probably already worried about us."

Danny took another bite out of his sandwich and waited.

And he waited.

It's not that Sara was ignoring Danny. She simply didn't hear a word he was saying. The reason was that she was completely fixed on the man walking on the other side of the lake. Sara couldn't take her eyes or her mind off of him. He had long brown hair and a beard and he was wearing a white robe with a dark red mantle. This was Jesus. That much was plain to Sara.

Finally, Danny heard a word from her lips: "There," she said.

"What?"

"There. Do you see him?" she asked.

"Who?"

"It's Jesus," said Sara.

"Where?"

"Over there. Across the lake."

Danny looked but saw no one.

"Do you see him?" she asked.

"No," said Danny.

Sara saw Jesus clearly. She pointed at him. "No, he's right there, standing on the other side of the lake. Can't you see him?"

"No."

"Really?" she asked.

Now Butch suddenly barked. And he, too, was staring out at the lake. Danny looked at him askance. "Can the dog see him, too?" he thought. "Give me a break."

"Nah!" said Danny. "I know you're just messing with me. I don't see him because there is no one there. Jesus is not here, Sara."

Suddenly it started to rain. Drops of water landed on the sparrow's head.

"We've got to go, Sara."

Suddenly Sara felt an electric tickle down her spine and the dead sparrow, which was still in her hands, started flapping its wings in a flurry; Sara immediately threw it into the sky and the bird flew up and away. Like any other bird in the forest. And all the while, Butch barked and barked, as if in applause, with one of those typical retriever grins that look like genuine laughter. He turned and looked over his shoulder right at Danny and seemed to say, "See, I knew she was right." Or at least that's what Danny thought he meant.

In any case, Danny was stunned. He looked at his sister in amazement. "That was so cool! How did you do that?"

"I didn't," she said. "He did it." Sara pointed across the lake, where she watched Jesus slowly turn and fade into the woods.

Danny just shook his head, uncomprehending. "I didn't see anyone."

Sara just smiled kindly at Danny. "We should go back to Grandpa's."

But Danny couldn't let it go. He kept scanning the lake, then looked back at Sara. "Did you really see Jesus?"

"Yes," she said.

"Then why couldn't I see him?"

Sara thought about it and finally just shrugged. "You saw the bird."

Danny looked at her quizzically and wrinkled his nose. "Yeah, I know, I saw it, but how come I couldn't see Jesus?"

Sara just smiled at him and began walking to the bikes. "Maybe we can get Mom to bring us back next weekend."

Danny stared at her in such total amazement that he didn't realize that Butch was inhaling the sandwich Danny had left on the log. Sara had done some strange things before, but she'd never stumped him like this.

"That was just totally cool. Come on, how did you bring that bird back to life?"

"I told you. It was Jesus."

The two of them got on their bikes and pedaled on away with Butch tagging behind and Danny wondering whether his sweet little sister was pulling his leg or whether she really did see Jesus. Could that be? All he knew for sure was that sparrow had been very dead for a very long time – like several hours -- and then for some reason, somehow, it got up and flapped its wings and flew away like nothing happened. Coolest thing he'd ever seen.

CHAPTER 4

Back at Sam's ranch, Bonnie was washing dishes when the kids got in; the rain had stopped but they were, of course, soaked to the skin. While Bonnie processed that with a long hard look, Sara just stood in the kitchen door for a moment, but Danny immediately ran up and said, "Mom, Sara brought a dead bird back to life!"

"That's nice, honey," said Bonnie, continuing with the dishes.

"No, really," said Danny breathlessly, "it was really cool and she said she saw Jesus."

"Yes, Danny, let me finish the dishes and you can tell me all about it," said Bonnie.

"Okay," said Danny. Then he held up the four trout he had caught. "By the way, I caught 'em so you can clean 'em. And can you cook the big one for me?"

"Well, thank you so much," said Bonnie. "And yes, I'll cook it for you, but first you take a shower and put on some dry clothes. You'll find them in the guest bedroom."

"Mom, I don't want to."

"And I don't want to clean the fish and cook them," said Bonnie, "but I will." And she looked at Danny pointedly.

"Okay, I'll take a shower," said Danny. He started running upstairs.

"Mom, where's Grandpa?" Sara asked.

"He's in the backyard," said Bonnie, but you go get into some dry clothes first."

"Yes, Mom, I will."

Later, Sara was out back, watching Grandpa Sam swing an axe and split a log. Sam glanced at Sara as he raised the axe.

"Catch any fish?" he asked.

"No," said Sara.

"Then you'd better tell your mother to take out some frozen meat and put it in the microwave."

"Danny caught four fish," she said.

Sam lowered the axe and looked at her. "And you didn't catch any? That doesn't sound like you."

"I found a dead bird."

"What did you do with it?"

"I set him free."

"If he was dead," Sam said, "I would say he was already about as free as he's ever going to be."

"No, Grandpa. He was alive when I let him go."

"Okay, I'm getting a little old," said Sam as he raised the axe and slammed it down to split a log in half. "Either that or I've got to get my hearing checked. I have no idea what you're trying to say."

Sara set about patiently explaining. "When I found the bird, I prayed. Then I saw Jesus standing on the other side of the lake and the bird flapped his wings and I let him go."

Sam put the axe-head on the ground and leaned on the handle as he smiled at his granddaughter. Partly he was smiling because of the surprising pleasure he felt at her story: weird as it was, it seemed somehow fitting, with it happening up on "his" lake and everything. "I always figured that place was kind of special," he said. "Always figured you were kind of special, too. How long were you praying?"

"All day."

"You are an amazing little girl, Sara."

Sara smiled. She loved being praised by her Grandpa.

"Did you tell your mother about this?" he asked.

"No, but Danny did."

"What did she say?"

"Not much. I don't think she believed him," said Sara.

"I can understand that," Sam said. "And you know, it might be wise to keep that story to yourself. A lot of people aren't as smart as I am. Most will figure you're making it up."

"But I'm telling the truth!" exclaimed Sara.

Sam put another log in front of him, raised the axe and split the log in two. "I know that, Darlin'. You coming back next weekend?"

"If Mom will bring us."

"I'll talk to her."

"Grandpa," she said, "are you ever going to get married again?"

Sam chuckled. "Did your mother tell you to ask me that?"

"No."

"Well, the way I reckon it," Sam said, "God gave me your grandmother who put up with me for a long time and that was more than I deserved. Somehow, I don't figure I should push the issue."

"You look young for a grandpa," said Sara.

"And you," Sam tapped his chest with his right hand above the heart, "look so beautiful that it makes my heart beat fast."

"Oh, Grandpa! Not really!"

Sam got on one knee and looked her in the eyes. "Yes, really." And Sara knew he meant it.

Then he stretched his hands as far as he could stretch them. "And I love you this much!"

Sara then stretched her hands as far as she could. "And I love you this much and even more!"

Sam then picked her up in his arms and said, "Let's go in the house and figure out how much that actually is!"

Bonnie fried the trout lightly in butter and olive oil with a little pepper and herbs in the simple Italian way her mother had taught her and served it with some sautéed spinach and tomatoes from Sam's garden. The kids loved it as much as she and Sam did. Meals at Grandpa's were always a good time. And Sara followed Grandpa's advice and though Danny kept waiting for her to bring it up, she kept mum about the bird and Jesus.

Later that night, as the kids waved good-bye to Grandpa

from the back seat of the Explorer, he stood on the porch and watched Bonnie drive them away. As the SUV rolled down the highway into the night, Danny couldn't stand it any more, leaned over the front seat and said simply, "Mom, Sara really did bring the bird back to life."

Bonnie just sighed as she drove. "I believe you both. And I know you think the bird was dead, but I'm sure it was only unconscious. As for the man by the lake, he was probably a hiker with a beard. I know you think he was wearing a red robe of some sort, but it's not uncommon for hikers to wear red wool jackets."

Danny listened, thought, gave Sara a look, then turned back to his mother. "Okay, well, I didn't see Jesus or a hiker, but that bird was dead. He didn't have a heartbeat."

"How do you know the bird was dead?" asked Bonnie.

"Because I couldn't see its heart beating."

"Is your heart still beating?" Bonnie asked.

"Yes, of course."

"Then why can't I see it beating?" said Bonnie.

Danny glanced down at his chest for a moment. "I... I don't know. Because you're driving?"

"Danny!"

"Just kidding."

"Now listen," she said. "I don't want to hear anything else about the bird or Sara seeing Jesus in the woods. Okay?"

Sara and Danny exchanged glances and for a few moments the silence just rang through the SUV.

"Did you hear me?" said Bonnie.

The kids replied as a chorus: "Yes, Mom."

So Bonnie had secured order. For the moment. And the rest of the ride home was very quiet indeed. But Bonnie knew from the start that this would be but a short silence and would not be the end of the subject. And she knew that Danny and Sara knew it, too.

That night as Bonnie tucked Sara in, she sat on Sara's bed and gave her a hug.

"Did you brush your teeth and floss?"

"Yes."

As Bonnie brushed Sara's hair, she said, "You have to go to school tomorrow, so say your prayers and get some sleep."

"Mom?"

Bonnie stopped and looked at her.

"It wasn't a hiker. And he spoke to me."

Bonnie knew something like this was coming, but the part about being spoken to surprised her.

"What did he say?"

"He said he'd be taking me to heaven soon."

Bonnie found herself taking a little deeper breath. "Honey, you can't go to heaven unless you die."

Sara looked up and pondered the ceiling a moment. "I don't want to die. But I want to go to heaven."

Bonnie maintained her cool but her heart pounded a little faster and brow furrowed. "Sara, you're letting your imagination run away with you and I don't want to ever lose you. You've got plenty of time to get to heaven. And when you go, you'll be a lot older than I am right now. Okay?"

Sara looked at her mom and seemed to process the idea. But really, Sara couldn't understand why her Mom was objecting to her being with Jesus. Yes, she'd have to leave, but isn't that the best place for anyone to be? With Jesus? Isn't that what they were teaching in church? Adults could be so complicated sometimes.

"Now you need to get some sleep. You have school tomorrow."

"I know. Can we go back to Grandpa's next weekend?"

"If you quit making up these stories."

Sara knew nothing she could say to that would make a difference, so she put her head on the pillow and stared at the ceiling.

Bonnie sat on Sara's bed and her eyes lingered on Sara for the longest moment by the moonlight coming in through the sheer curtains. "This is my daughter," she thought, and she had to fight panic as she realized: "I have no idea what's going on with her." And for that moment, time stood still and she found herself flashing on the path she had taken to arrive at this place and time. She very nearly didn't get here.

CHAPTER 5

For one thing, it wasn't easy being Sam Donovan's daughter in this town. While growing up, Bonnie often couldn't wait to leave. There was a while in her youth when Sam had hoped he could groom her to take over the horse ranch. He had this fantasy that she would love the quarter horses and Arabians as much as he did and that she maybe would take up riding competitively and maybe try for the Olympics team in dressage or jumping. After all, she was so pretty and so athletic. But, try to please him though she did in every way she could think of, the equestrian world was never really her cup of tea and she felt she had disappointed him mightily.

Then there was the period when, many years after fact, Sam began having battlefield flashbacks, or as they now called it, "post-traumatic stress disorder." He dealt with it at the time mostly with Tequila and the produce of his vintner neighbors. This went very hard on Bonnie and her mother, Rachel. Bonnie always loved him, was restless to prove herself to him somehow, but he was sometimes, oh, so scary to be around.

Then when Bonnie was eighteen, her mother, Rachel, in the family pickup, loaded with groceries just bought in the village, made a turn onto the highway and she didn't see the semi-trailer truck coming through the orange groves at a crossroads. Nor could she have known that its brakes had failed. She was broadsided, totaling the pickup and killing her instantly. Bonnie was devastated.

Leaving for UCLA was a mercy; she thought she'd never return. When she did come back, she never thought she'd stay, not in this place full of grief and backward ways and winding roads that would take her nowhere. Then after she married and settled here with Alex, she promised herself that when the kids got a little older they would move. Far away. Until finally it all came to a head one long weekend.

She took a trip to see some friends in Los Angeles, to her old college haunts. Well, through an old friend she had a stunning stroke of good fortune: she found out about a high-paying engineering job at an aerospace company in the South Bay that would be perfect for her husband. She even found a house they could afford in Culver City. She couldn't wait to get back to tell Alex about it. Bonnie determined to surprise him. She hired a baby sitter and took Alex out to dinner in White Dove at the Trattoria Roma, their favorite Italian place, the kind with white tablecloths. She planned to make a big presentation about the job and show him pictures of the house. She was so excited. She just couldn't wait to finally move and leave this town behind.

Then the food arrived. She had ordered the Brodeto Dei Pescadori Al Xaferan, a traditional Italian seafood and vegetable stew. She took one taste of a scallop with the saffron and garlic in white wine and suddenly she was back in her mother's kitchen. Then she thought, why shouldn't she feel that way? It was her cousin, Richie, who owned this restaurant. Guess where he got his recipes? But to Bonnie this was true comfort food. As the meal progressed, she found herself thinking a new thought, changing focus. Why? It was more than the food. What was it? She could feel something slowly turning her, changing her mind. Was it her husband across the table enjoying her company even more than his dinner? Was it the waiters, the ambiance? But what does that mean? As she looked around the restaurant, she began to see things. Two tables over, there sat her neighbors, the Papadakis' from down the street; their kids played with Danny and Sara all the time. On the other side, enjoying his chicken cacciatore was Dr. David Riley, the Hopkins family's doctor; his wife, Elizabeth, was having some tasty-looking mushroom ravioli – not really items on her diet as she continued to struggle with her weight, but, well, it was only once a week and she loved it so much. She really knew how to enjoy life. And then walking through the front door came ninety-year-old Mrs. Maggie Elliott Steiner, Bonnie's high school English teacher, still spry as ever, wearing her signature Birkenstocks, and spreading greetings and sunshine to one and all in the room.

"Hello, Bonnie Dear," said Mrs. Steiner. "How are Danny and Sara doing?"

"Just wonderful, Mrs. Steiner, and how are you?"

"I feel great! And right now, I am as hungry as a horse."

Mrs. Steiner sat down with her sixty-five year-old son, Arnold Steiner, ordered a bottle of White Dove Valley Chardonnay with her garlic chicken and angel hair pasta and pretty much held court throughout the evening as a number of people came up to her table and paid their respects.

"You know, that lady," Bonnie said quietly to Alex, "probably taught English to like half the people in this room."

"That would figure," said Alex.

"And she knows just about everybody in town."

Alex smiled at his wife, "Yeah, kind of like you."

Bonnie then took another look around the room, thought about all she had been through, and realized Alex was right. The people in this room, the people in this town, were the people she had known all her life, and more than that, this beautiful, slow-moving, backward little village was an inseparable part of what made her happy. She suddenly had a palpable sense of how perfectly she fit into White Dove and of how it was easy to do.

And why not? The only things that everyone had agreed to forbid here was pretense and prejudice. That and chain stores; they had to stay outside the city limits. That's why so many businesses in town had been owned by local families for generations. This wasn't the kind of small town where you just passed through. It was the kind of place where you felt you had arrived. Tucked away in the end of a hidden valley, the town was an anomaly, a kind of Shangri-la with a fierce tradition of independence. A beautiful place, where life was slow and comfortable. And there were hot springs in the valley dating from Indian times, so this was a spa town where magnates and moguls came to retire among the surrounding vineyards and citrus orchards. But to be happy here, you had to leave your façade behind when you came. There was something about the place that demanded authenticity and also made it easy to achieve. For over a century, this was the one place where it was an aggressively held social compact among the locals to regard individuals for themselves and their character alone and not their background or circumstances. And no one cared if you were black or white or green or purple, and anyone could share the sidewalk with an orange picker or a movie star or a housewife or a surgeon, or indeed the town drunk, and never care about nor even notice the difference.

Suddenly it all made sense to Bonnie and in that moment she felt a huge feeling of relief. For maybe the first time in her life, she realized that she was truly home.

"So tell me about your trip to L.A.," said Alex.

"Well, uh... it was great. I feel like I was guided."

"How do you mean?" asked Alex with a grin. "Like by GPS?"

"Yeah, maybe," laughed Bonnie, "but maybe more, and you know, I really learned a lot."

"How so?"

"I learned," said Bonnie with simple reflection, "I learned how much I missed my family." That was a moment she would always remember. That was the moment everything changed. Among other things, she felt it made her a stronger mother.

But now, there Bonnie sat on Sara's bed, staring into her daughter's eyes, trying to fathom her mind. Bonnie thought, "On the one hand it's probably some freak childhood thing that will pass, but on the other, I am desperately fighting the recognition that she's scaring the hell out me."

Bonnie hugged her daughter heartily and kissed her on the forehead.

"Yes, Honey, then maybe it was Jesus," said Bonnie. "My little angel. But I won't let him take you to heaven just yet."

Sara beamed at her mother with contentment. "Can we go to Grandpa's again next weekend?"

"If you take me to the place where you saw this dead bird and Jesus."

"Okay."

Bonnie tucked Sara in with a kiss on the cheek. Tomorrow was Monday -- a school day -- and even little angels in the third grade need their sleep.

Later that evening, when Bonnie shared her feelings of angst with Alex, he said, "Yes, but isn't this kind of – what? – whimsy? – this kind of imagination -- part of what makes Sara the wondrous child she is? And, in fact, the natural extension and next step beyond her mother?"

"Wow," said Bonnie. "That may turn out to be the most terrifying thing about this whole parenthood thing: when you realize that your kids will go beyond you."

Alex nodded, "They'll go past our reach and past everything we expect in every way. Isn't that what we did growing up? We can't control or predict even the smallest aspect of their lives. We can only love them and teach them and pray, and hope that they turn out in a way that leaves them happy and content."

The Hopkins didn't sleep too well that night.

CHAPTER 6

The next morning Bonnie and Alex were awakened by Danny knocking on their bedroom door. He came in and announced that he thought Sara was sick.

"What'd you say, Honey?" asked Bonnie.

Alex raised his head. "What's wrong with Sara?"

"I don't know," said Danny. "When I got up and went to the bathroom, I heard her moaning in her room. I went in and she's covered in sweat."

Some thirty minutes later, Dr. David Riley had arrived and was sitting by Sara's bed with his black medical satchel parked on her nightstand on top of a scattered array of art pencils and sketch-pads. She sat on the edge of the bed as he moved his stethoscope down her chest.

He asked, "How are you feeling right now?"

"Not good. I don't feel good at all. I feel really sick. Really, really sick."

"Okay, let's see what we can do to make you feel better."

As he reached out and touched her forehead, little Sara violently threw up all over Dr. Riley. And this was no minor burp. This was some serious projectile vomiting. He stood up and stepped back, and looked down at his suit covered in yellow puke.

"I'm sorry."

"It's okay, Sara," said the Doctor.

"I think I feel a little better now," she said.

"I'm so glad I could help."

Later that morning Alex and Bonnie stood on their driveway with Dr. Riley, who was now wearing some of Alex's clothes as he carried his suit in a plastic bag.

"I'm sorry about your clothes," said Bonnie. "Can I have them dry cleaned?"

"No, these things go with the job, but you can come by and pick up Alex's clothes tomorrow."

"Is Sara going to be okay?" asked Bonnie.

"She's going to be fine," said the Doctor. "It's the stomach flu. It's going around. Keep her home for a day or two and keep her hydrated."

Bonnie hesitated a moment as she shared a look with Alex, who nodded to her to go ahead. "It's just that something she said scared me."

"What was that?"

"Well," said Bonnie, "she thinks that she saw Jesus at the lake when we were visiting my dad. And she says she brought a dead bird back to life. I don't know what to make of it, but actually, Danny says he saw her do that. So I'm really confused."

Dr. Riley nodded carefully. "Well, that's unusual certainly, but we know she is a very, uh, imaginative child and probably very impressionable, but I'm not sure you need to worry a lot about it."

"Yeah, but then she said something else.... She said that Jesus spoke to her. And what he told her... what he told her was that... he would be taking her to heaven soon."

The Doctor just held her gaze for a moment. He didn't let loose any of the thoughts that ran riot in his head; no rant about the absurdity of mysticism and the futility of belief in miracles and apparitions. No, Dr. Riley was a pro. And it helped that he had genuine compassion for Bonnie and Alex. "She's going to be just fine," he said to Bonnie. "Sara is healthier than you or I and will outlive us both."

Alex put his arm around Bonnie and smiled. "See, I told you everything is going be good."

Bonnie nodded half-heartedly and thanked the Doctor for coming.

"If it gets any worse," said Dr. Riley, "or if anything happens, call my office."

Later, as that night unfolded at the Hopkins house and the moon shadows moved from her pillow to the cross above Sara's bed, Alex's optimism began to seem warranted, because although Sara's parents only tried to sleep, the little girl herself fell into a slumber that was peaceful and deep.

CHAPTER 7

White Dove was the kind of town where most people preferred to walk or bike whenever possible and the elementary school was only three blocks from the Hopkins' home. So Sara and Danny would usually walk, as they did this day, coming homeward down the oak-tree-lined neighborhood streets alongside the Miller kids: Ellen, a tall twelve-year-old, and Sylvia, age nine. Sara carried a large Manila envelope as she walked next to the wheel-bound Mark. He had grown pretty adept with his power-cart since the crash two years ago. Everyone said he had come a long way. At first he wasn't expected to live, then the doctors were surprised that he could get around so well in his chair. They seemed surprised no matter he accomplished, but Mark never paid them any mind. He had a life to live and he just knew what he wanted and held on to a belief that he could find a way to make it happen.

Sara handed Mark the Manila envelope. "Here, I made something for you."

Mark was surprised and even more so when he opened it. The contents? An extremely well-drawn picture of Mark flying through the air and executing a dramatic slam-dunk.

Mark was blown away. "Sara, how?"

She shrugged. "I've always been able to draw."

"But this is unbelievable! I'm going to hang it in my bedroom."

He reached out and squeezed her hand, as they smiled at each other. "Thank you, Sara."

Three boys from Danny's class rode up next to the group on bicycles. Tommy Higgins, a freckle-faced, red-haired kid, pedaled up to them and said, "Hey, Sara, my dog died last week. I was wondering if you could stop by and bring him back to life for me?"

Sara looked at Tommy with a stunned expression then turned her gaze to Danny, who avoided her look. He knew he was in trouble now.

Then a second bike boy, Denny Valenzuela, said to Sara, "Hey, my frog died last night. Could you stop by and bring him back to life?"

"If you see Jesus," said Tommy, "tell him we said Hi."

"Yeah," said the third bicyclist, Carter Jackson, "We're having a party this weekend. Could you bring Jesus by? Maybe he could turn some water into wine for us?"

Sarah, of course, didn't respond, she just looked straight ahead and kept walking. Then all three of the boys cracked up in hysterical laughter and pedaled away, hooting and shouting and generally having a hilarious time.

"I'm sorry," said Danny, "It was just so cool. I had to tell someone."

"Like everyone, right?" said Sara.

"Well, uh... yeah, pretty much."

Sara just shook her head.

Mark Miller rolled up to Sara in his chair. "Sara," he said, "Forget about those guys. They're idiots and everyone knows it."

Mark's sister Ellen chimed in: "Mark is right. Those three are just stupid clowns."

"You know, I heard the story, too. Did you really see Jesus?" Mark asked. "Did a dead bird really come back to life?"

Sara looked up and saw that Mark and his sisters were hanging on the answer.

"Yes," said Sara.

"Wow, that's really cool," said Mark.

So the five of them continued another block and a half, with Danny chatting up the sisters on either side of him in front, followed by Sara and Mark. Danny combed his hair as they went and the girls by their smiles seemed to approve. Soon they found themselves in front of the Miller house.

Sylvia said, "You can come in if you want."

Danny looked at Sara, who said, "I think we need to get home."

Danny turned to Sylvia. "Maybe tomorrow?" Danny said.

"I'd like that," said Sylvia.

Danny reflexively took out his comb and ran it through his wave. The two girls looked at each other and giggled.

Mark said to Sara, "Do you want to walk with us tomorrow?"

"Sure," said Sara.

Then, as she and Danny started to walk away, Mark yelled out, "Sara, could you come here a moment?" Sara turned and walked back to Mark, who then reached out, took her schoolbooks, put them in his lap and then held her hands.

"Sara, could you do something for me?" Immediately Sara felt the electric tickle down her spine and it startled her. Still holding her hands, Mark said, "Could you say a prayer for me?"

Sara closed her eyes and prayed silently for a moment. When she opened her eyes, she said, "I'll pray more when I get home."

"Thanks. See you tomorrow."

Sara nodded okay. After the goodbyes were complete and Danny had combed his hair yet again and the Millers were safely inside, and Sara and Danny walked on homeward, Danny asked her, "What were you doing back there?"

"I said a prayer for him."

A very wide grin came across Danny's face: "You're so cool!" Sara just shrugged and they kept on walking.

CHAPTER 8

And so another day dawned over White Dove. At the lake the tree-shadows moved with the rising of the light, while the deer and the coyotes and pumas retired to their daytime homes deep in the brush and left the shores of the crystalline lake to the mallards and the transient Canada geese. In town, the villagers started to move about their day and what passed for traffic in the little town began to bustle down White Dove Avenue.

Dr. David Riley sat in his office going over his schedule of patients for the day with his Nurse, Anna Suarez, who noticed through the window that Flo Miller had just pulled her weathered van into the parking lot and began unloading Mark's motor-chair via the electric lift gate.

"Oh my," said Anna. "Mark Miller wasn't on the schedule. Something must have happened. That poor boy."

Dr. Riley sighed and shook his head. Mark was one of his favorite patients. He'd known the Millers most of his life and Mark since he was born. Ever since the accident, the Doctor had agonized over Mark's treatment and therapy. He wanted to give him hope, but in his heart he knew that there was no way Mark's upbeat attitude could make up for the serious destruction of nerve tissue he had experienced.

As Anna led Flo and Mark into an examination room, she couldn't help noticing that they carried a sense of tension – but oddly – there was nothing negative about it, like you'd expect to see in an emergency room. Rather it was a sense of bursting expectation.

Dr. Riley entered and said, "Flora, how are you?"

"I'm great!" she said, with strangely manic energy and volume that stunned Dr. Riley a bit. "How are you?!"

"I, uh, I'm fine," said Dr. Riley. "So tell me, what's this emergency visit all about?"

Flora nodded to Mark. "This morning," said Mark, "I moved my toes."

Dr. Riley's jaw hung open as he hesitated a moment. "If you did that," he said, "it would be incredible. Do you think you could show me?"

"Sure"

Dr. Riley squatted down and took off both of Mark's shoes. "Let's see what you can do."

Mark began to strain. Nothing happened.

"Just wait," Mark said, "I'll try again."

Mark strained again and still nothing. Flo just sat and held her breath with her hand over her mouth.

"I'm sorry, Mark," said Dr. Riley, "but the nerve in your spine was severed in the accident and nerves can't – "

Mark cut him off: "Let me try again."

Mark started straining again. And this time his right big toe moved. Followed by the others. Then the left foot. It took a few minutes but result was the same. All of his toes moved.

Dr. Riley's jaw dropped. "Can you do that again, Mark?"

Mark strained again, and again the toes moved and Dr. Riley was more confused than ever. But Mark wasn't through. Now he lifted his whole foot an inch off the wheel chair's footrest. Dr. Riley was beyond astonishment.

"That's amazing! Could you try and do that one more time?"

Mark strained a bit and then lifted the foot again – this time with seemingly less effort.

"Wow," said Dr. Riley, blowing out his breath. "I need to talk to your mother for a moment and then schedule you for some more tests." And he was beaming at Mark. "You did very well, Mark. That was amazing."

Then Dr. Riley remembered he had a practice to run. "I have another patient I need to see." He turned to Flora: "Could you walk to the waiting room with me? I want Anna to schedule some tests at the hospital. I've never seen anything like this."

The Doctor and Flora went into the hallway and he said to her quietly, "Now listen, Flora, I don't want you to get overly excited yet."

"I understand," said Flora. "You know, I'm suddenly so scared."

"Why is that?"

"This is the first time in years we've had any hope at all and now it's here," she said. "What if that hope is taken away from us?"

"Flora, I think your instincts are correct. On the one hand you need to be strong for Mark, but on the other, you can't get your hopes up. You've got to understand, this does not mean he'll walk again. I can't explain what happened in there, but this is really basic: for one thing, nerves grow very slowly in the best of circumstances, but severed nerves in the spinal cord just cannot regenerate. Period. This is very unusual. Something is going on here, but... please don't get your hopes too high. I'm happy to see the progress, but I'm very surprised. I will do a CT scan and some other tests at the hospital. Do you think you could take Mark there this afternoon?"

"Of course," said Flora. In the waiting room, as Dr. Riley handed the prescription for Mark's test to Anna, Flora saw a young, thirty-ish woman wave at the doctor.

"Is that Dolores Clark, the news lady from Channel 14?" Flora asked.

"Yes," said Dr. Riley. "She's one of my patients."

Then from behind them, they heard Mark calling. "Mom, Dr. Riley!"

They turned around to see Mark walking into the waiting room. Slowly and with great effort, but he was actually walking!

"Oh, my God" said Flora, "You're walking!" She rushed to her son and held him as tears flowed down both their faces. And Dr. Riley was now totally gob-smacked, as his Irish great-grandfather would have put it. He hadn't the slightest clue what was going on here.

Dolores Clark got up from her chair and approached the Doctor. "That's the Miller boy," she said. "I did the story on him when he was hit by the car. I thought he was never supposed to walk again."

"He wasn't."

Mark stepped over toward Dr. Riley and Dolores and said, "It was Sara. Sara Hopkins. She speaks with Jesus. She brought a bird back to life and now she's healed me."

"You're talking about Alex and Bonnie's little girl?" asked Dolores.

"Yes," Mark nodded.

That was enough for Dolores. She turned and headed for the door.

Dr. Riley yelled after her, "Dolores, I know where you're going and what you're thinking. Don't do this!"

"Are you kidding?" Dolores said. "When a little girl brings a bird back to life and then heals a paralyzed boy who was never supposed to walk again – like that's not news?"

"Let's get the facts first," said Dr. Riley.

"I just did," said Dolores. "You said he was never supposed to walk again." And Dolores strode out of the building, leaving Dr. Riley shaking his head and looking perturbed.

CHAPTER 9

"I think Sylvia likes me," said Danny as the family sat at dinner.

"I think she would like you more," said Sara, "if you didn't comb your hair so much."

Danny smirked at her. "Well, I think Mark likes you."

Sara smiled. "I like him, too."

"No, I mean like Sylvia likes me."

Sara just rolled her eyes and shrugged. She had no idea what Danny was going on about. But it didn't bother her since she found herself responding that way to a lot of Danny's comments. She thought maybe this was just what brothers did.

Then the doorbell rang. Alex finished his peach cobbler, got up and answered the door to let in Dr. Riley and Pastor Jenkins.

"Mom," said Sara, "you didn't have to call the doctor. I told you I was feeling better."

"We're here on another matter, Sara," said Pastor Jenkins with one eye on Bonnie. "We were wondering if we might talk to you?"

"It's about the bird, isn't it?" Danny chimed in.

Bonnie said to Danny, "You can go in the family room and play Nintendo or watch TV if you want."

"Aw, Mom!" came the plaintive wail.

"It's okay," said the Pastor. "He can stay."

"Gentlemen, please have a seat," said Bonnie

As Bonnie, Alex and Danny cleared the dishes, the Doctor sat at the table next to Sara. But first he turned to Danny and said, "You know, I actually would like to hear more about this bird, but something else happened at my office today that I'd like to talk to Sara about."

"What happened?" asked Sara.

"Well, before we get into that," said Dr. Riley, "since we're here, I'll have a look at you." He feels her forehead, checks her eyes. "How do you feel?"

"I feel better."

"And what were you feeling before?"

"I had a headache and I was really tired when I came home yesterday. And today I've been tired all day. I'm feeling a little better now."

"Maybe you still have a touch of the flu," said Dr. Riley. "But I think we should have your mother bring you to the office tomorrow."

"I don't want to miss any more school."

"She can bring you in after school."

"Okay," said Sara.

"Now, Sara," said the Doctor, "when was the last time you saw Mark Miller?"

"Yesterday. We walked him home after school."

Pastor Jenkins asked her, "Did anything happen? Anything unusual?"

"No. Well, he asked me to pray for him. So I closed my eyes and asked Jesus to heal him. Why? What happened?"

The Pastor said, "Mark Miller came into Dr. Riley's office today and he... he got up and walked."

Sara's face lit up into a huge smile and she clapped her hands. "That's great! I'm so happy!"

Bonnie and Alex were, of course, astonished at the news.

"Then he's okay?" asked Sara.

"Yes," said Pastor Jenkins. "He seems to have made a full recovery, as far as we can tell at this point. We were just wondering if you could tell us anything about that?"

"I didn't do anything," said Sara. "I just held his hands and prayed for him."

The Pastor shared a glance with the Doctor, who looked so serious he was almost pained.

"And could you tell me about what happened at the lake the other day?" the Pastor continued. "Mark Miller said you brought a bird back to life and saw Jesus. Is that true?"

"No," said Sara.

Everyone at the table looked at her. Dr. Riley shared a moment's glance with the Pastor as if to say, with some relief, ah, so it's not true after all. There must be some "natural" explanation.

Then Sara continued: "I saw Jesus, but I didn't bring the bird back to life. Jesus did."

So Dr. Riley had to think again. Pastor Jenkins now turned to Danny. "I understand you were with your sister when this happened?"

Danny sat up straight, put on his best suave look and ran the ever-present comb through his hair. "I caught four fish at the lake. Sara had the dead bird in her hand and she asked if I could see Jesus. I said no. A moment later the bird came to life and flew away. It was way cool."

"So you did not see Jesus, then?" said Pastor Jenkins.

"No," said Danny, "but I saw the bird come back to life."

Dr. Riley then asked, "Sara, when you saw Jesus, did he speak to you?"

"Yes."

"Do you speak to Jesus often?"

"All the time, Doctor. Don't you?"

"No."

"Not even in Church?"

"The Doc is more like me, Sara," said Danny, cheerfully butting in. "It's not that we don't believe in him, we just know he's busy and we don't want to take up too much of his time. Do we, Doc? Just kind of let him do his own thing, right?"

Danny then pulled out his comb, ran it through his hair and smiled at Dr. Riley, who appeared a little sheepish, unsure of just how to react to all this. Bonnie on the other hand had no such uncertainty.

"Take your Nintendo game and go play it in the family room," said Bonnie. Danny looked reluctant. "Move it."

"Okay, Mom," said Danny as he shuffled out of the room.

Dr. Riley had by now collected himself. "Sara, I'm not

telling you not to pray," he said. "What I am saying is, it's not healthy to pretend you are actually having conversations with Jesus."

"I don't pretend," said Sara.

Dr. Riley nodded his professional nod and stood up, ready to leave as he looked over at Bonnie and Alex. "You should bring her by the office tomorrow afternoon. With the fatigue and headaches and, uh...well, at her age... that needs to be examined."

As the Doctor headed for the door escorted by Bonnie and Alex, the Pastor said, "I'll be out in a moment. I'd just like to have a word with Sara. Just the two of us."

As the others exited the room, the Pastor leaned his elbows on the table and cupped his face in his hands as he leaned closer to Sara. "Honey," he said slowly and earnestly, "are you really sure that you saw Jesus at the lake?"

Sara, a little puzzled by the intensity of the Pastor, just nodded her head yes.

"Did your brother see him, too?"

Sara shook her head no. "Danny already answered that question for them," she thought, "Could they not be paying attention?"

"Did anything else happen while you were at the lake?"

Now Sara smiled. "It rained chickens and ducks."

The Pastor inclined his head. "Now that's an expression I've never heard before."

"Because it's 'fowl' weather. That's what Grandpa calls it."

It took the Pastor a moment or two, but he finally smiled and laughed a quiet laugh. "I get it," he chuckled, "chickens, ducks. Fowl weather. I get it. That's funny."

Sara had a big grin on her face. She liked making people laugh.

By the time Pastor Jenkins got outside to where Dr. Riley was taking to the Hopkins, no one was laughing.

"You've got to talk to her," said Dr. Riley to Bonnie and Alex. "These stories about healing birds and making crippled boys walk are going to turn her life into a media circus. Yours as well.

"Doctor," asked Alex, "is there an explanation for Mark's recovery?"

"Absolutely. I can assure you there is a logical explanation for it."

"However," the Pastor chimed in, "at the moment we haven't the faintest idea what that is."

Dr. Riley was getting annoyed with his old friend. "Bob, don't be pouring fuel on the fire. Sara doesn't need that."

"Look," said Pastor Jenkins, "I can't claim to know exactly what has happened here, but I do know that Sara believes everything she's telling us."

"She does have an imagination," said Bonnie, "but she has never outright lied. She wouldn't do that."

Dr. Riley nodded earnestly. "Let's just try and keep this among ourselves until we get to the bottom of it. Right now, I'm worried about her headaches and her fatigue."

Bonnie then agreed to bring her by the Doctor's office the next day after school.

Later that night, the Doctor's 5-year-old Mercedes E250 arrived in front of Pastor Jenkins' rectory. As the two men sat a moment, each reflecting on this strange day, Pastor Jenkins turned to him and said, "You have to open up your mind, David. Unless you have an explanation for what happened to Mark."

"I can't explain it yet. But there's a great deal I don't yet know about the case and I am certain we will find a logical explanation."

"What if it was a divine miracle?"

"I... let's just say I don't believe in miracles," said Dr. Riley, "divine or otherwise."

"I do," said the Pastor.

"And if you convince everyone else in town to believe in them," said the Doctor, "what's going to happen to Sara?"

Clearly Pastor Jenkins hadn't thought much about that. He got out of the car. Then he had a notion. He bent over and put his head in the window. "I think if your son were here – "

"Leave Jesse out of this," said Dr. Riley, cutting him off.

"David," said the Pastor, "you come to church every Sunday. Why?"

Dr. Riley shrugged. "It makes Elizabeth feel better."

Bob Jenkins knew the Doctor about as well as anyone did. These men had grown up together in this town, ever since David's father, the famous Al Riley, wrapped up his career as an outfielder with the San Francisco Giants in the early 1970's and bought an avocado ranch here in the Valley. It was old Pastor Bob, Sr., who had convinced him to do that. They had met ten years earlier at Martin Luther King's March on Washington. Al found in old Bob a kindred spirit and he found in White Dove a place that for the most part was already living the dream of equality that the good Dr. King had preached about on that memorable, steamy, August day in 1963 before so many thousands at the reflecting pool in front of the Lincoln Memorial. So as an African-American, young David Riley grew up in a place of exceptional and fortunate nurture in so many ways.

Yet now, as Bob looked hard and deep at his old friend, that sense of security seemed to have gone from him. "You know, David, God hasn't deserted you, but I'm wondering, have you deserted God?"

And they just stared at each other until they both realized it was not a question David Riley was prepared to answer, as it was not a perspective that had ever occurred to him.

Jesse Riley had just reached his eighteenth birthday when he passed. A more perfect son David could not have dreamed of. Handsome and athletic, Jesse was a star distance runner on the high school team and he was brilliant – accepted into both Columbia and Stanford. Wanted to be a doctor. Which David of course loved; what he didn't love was that Jesse was leaning toward Columbia, rather than David's alma mater, Stanford. This one crazy, petty difference became the occasion for a huge fight. They both said things they later regretted. Jesse stomped out of the house and went for a long run in the hills. An old rancher couple out for an evening stroll found Jesse on the trail, wearing his blue varsity track-suit, collapsed and in a coma. It was a sleep he would never awaken from. Four months later, when they buried him, as he and Elizabeth stood by the open grave and she broke down and wept openly, David found himself having to fight an irrational urge to follow his son and leap into the grave. That it even crossed his mind for an instant left him appalled and terrified. He never shared those feelings with anyone, not even Elizabeth. No, especially not Elizabeth; he had to be strong for her. But he wasn't so sure he could be strong for himself.

In the living room of their otherwise dark house, Elizabeth Riley was staring at the local TV news when her husband walked in, looking very exhausted. He immediately started taking off his jacket and shoes. It had been a long day.

"Did you see Sara?" she asked.

"Yes."

"And?"

"She's just a little girl," said David. "She thinks she saw Jesus and she thinks Jesus healed the boy."

David went into the den that served as his home office. As he unpacked his briefcase, Elizabeth followed and stood at the door.

"I know you're mad at him," said Elizabeth.

"Mad? At who?"

"At Jesus. At God," she said. "He was my son, too, David, but I'm not as strong as you. Because if I quit believing in God, I would have to believe that our son no longer exists. I can't do that. I'm just not that strong. I don't think you are either."

David sat at his desk and put his face in his hands. He found himself fighting the feeling that Jesse died just yesterday and the last twelve years never happened. As if he hadn't cursed himself twenty times a day since then for making his last words to his son words of anger. Yes, the feeling of wanting to dial it all back persisted and the futility of that wish only tormented David the more.

"Elizabeth, Sara is just a little girl. She doesn't need you and everyone else thinking she's an instrument of God."

"Why not? A little girl with faith? What's wrong with that? That's something we could use a little more of. Something the whole world could use a lot more of."

David looked up at his wife. "If there really is a God, do you think he would create a world where parents have to watch their sons and daughters die?"

"At my Doctor's office today, I witnessed a miracle," came the voice of Dolores Clark on the Channel 14 News, which continued on the TV. And of course, the Rileys stopped and watched. "I saw a ten-year-old boy who had been paralyzed from the waist down get up and walk," said Dolores on the tube.

CHAPTER 10

Across town in the Hopkins' house, Alex and Bonnie watched the same news program and were also rapt by Dolores Clark's report:

"The boy, Mark Miller of White Dove, said that Sara Hopkins, a third-grader from his elementary school, had held his hands and prayed for him. Now, I happen to attend church with both of these children, and I can tell you it is not hard for me to accept and believe what young Mark Miller said. But the real question is what do each of you believe?"

"Yeah, that's right," Alex said to the TV, "invite everybody to get involved. Let the circus begin." Alex was steamed; he suddenly turned the TV off. "I guess we'd better shut the blinds," he said. "The reporters will start crowding the front lawn pretty soon."

Bonnie's brow furrowed; she too found herself worrying that this could shape up as a media feeding-frenzy at the expense of Sara and the whole family.

A few blocks away, Maria de la Paz had a very different thought as she sat in her living room with her brother, Father Alanzo Echevarria, who was Catholic priest, visiting from Mexico, and the two of them, in astonishment, watched the Dolores Clark broadcast as well. They certainly had more than a passing fascination with the story, but it was not about the publicity. They didn't have to look at each other to share the same thought. Maria's daughter, Theresa, was dying of cancer. Could this little girl, Sara, who lived a few blocks away, be the answer?

While Maria and Alanzo watched the news, Theresa sat in her bedroom and played balero, the traditional Mexican cup and ball game. She tossed the cup on the string into the air and caught it on the handle. Then she did it again. And again. It was one of the ways she passed her time. There weren't many other play opportunities for a cancer patient; more complex or vigorous pursuits exhausted her quickly. This way she could lie back on her bed every few minutes and rest.

Smiling at Theresa from the doorway was Father Alanzo's young colleague who worked with him in Mexico, Father Bernardo Moretti. He had with him a cup and handle a little larger than the one Maria had, and the string that holds the cup was longer. He offered her the toy.

"I heard you like to play boliche," said Father Bernardo.

"You mean balero?" said Theresa shyly.

"Yes, that's what it's called in Mexico," said Father Bernardo. "In Spain we call it boliche. I thought you might enjoy this one. There's more you can do with it."

Father Bernardo demonstrated. He took the handle in one hand, the string in the other, made the cup do a flip in the air and then caught it on the handle. Theresa was intrigued as he did it four times without stopping.

Then Theresa tried it. At first she missed but after a few tries she was flipping it like a pro.

"That's fun," said Theresa, smiling up at him. "Thank you, Father Bernardo." Then she looked down at the balero and away from him. "I heard the doctor tell my mother that my cancer is getting worse," Theresa said. "He said I didn't have much time. Am I going to die?"

Father Bernardo was taken aback by her directness. "When did you hear this?" he asked.

"At the hospital today."

Father Bernardo found himself on the one hand admiring her courage and on the other he was totally at a loss for words. Theresa finally looked up at him.

"We don't have to talk about it if it upsets you," she said.

Father Bernardo sat next to her on the bed and put his arm around her. "It doesn't upset me, Theresa," he said. "We can talk about it."

"I'm just not sure what will happen to me when I die."

Father Bernardo Moretti was a very young priest. The son of a wealthy Italian diplomat, raised mostly in Spain, based now in the Vatican, he was thrilled to be working with the poor on a temporary assignment alongside Father Echevarria in Michoacan, in rural Mexico. But it was moments like this that brought home to him the true weight of the Sunday sermons he preached from the pulpit. There are crossroads all of us must face and make the right decisions or not. But this little girl had to face the journey of a lifetime at the age of eight. As a friend and a virtual uncle, and a priest, he knew he had to make sure she didn't have to face the journey alone.

"Jesus said," Father Bernardo began, "I am the resurrection and the life. He who believes in me will live, even though he dies; and whoever lives and believes in me will never die. Do you believe this?"

"I guess," Theresa said. "What does it mean?"

"It means that if you believe in Jesus, your body here on earth may die, but your soul will go to heaven where it will live with him forever."

Theresa thought about it a moment. "Will your soul go to heaven even if you're really scared of dying?"

"Yes," said Father Bernardo, "as long as you keep faith in Jesus."

"Okay," she said getting off the bed, "I'm going to go show mommy my new balero."

In the living room, Maria and her brother watched the news broadcast wrap-up. Besides Dolores Clark's initial report, she did several "man-on-the-street" interviews of random locals and finally she signed off with the assurance that she would "keep you up to date" on "The Miracles of Sara Hopkins."

Maria turned and asked Alanzo point-blank, "Do you think she could heal Theresa?"

Now, Alanzo knew what his heart wanted, but he also knew he had better speak carefully. He and Maria came from an old Spanish family known for a great-uncle several times removed, Thomas Echevarria, who in 1919 had been a priest in the Cantabria region of Northern Spain and who was associated with a series of miracles in which a church crucifix came to life on many occasions, causing widespread religious ecstasy. The Crucifix of Limpias was an internationally celebrated icon that, in its day, drew more visitors than Lourdes. With miracles being witnessed by princes and cardinals, as well as merchants and peasants and lawyers and atheists. There were testimonies by the thousands from all walks of life. What Alanzo found most fascinating was that each witness gave a unique account. Some saw the eyes closed, some saw them sweeping the room, some heard the Christ speak, some saw him sweat blood, some saw flowing tears, others saw the open sores and bruises, and for some the figure seemed to struggle to get off the cross. On some he gazed lovingly, to others he looked stern. Some witnesses were uplifted. Others could not stop weeping. Alanzo couldn't help inferring that this kind of communion with the Savior was, somehow, an inherently personal experience. Perspective seemed to be nearly everything. But he had to admit to himself, he found it all somewhat confusing.

In any event, this chapter of Alanzo's family history, which he was steeped in, was a catalyst that had inspired him to seek a position with the Congregation for the Causes of the Saints, the Vatican office tasked with investigating miracles, martyrdom and heroic virtues of various servants of God. He spent five years researching various claims of miracles. He found the task richly rewarding and enlightening, but finally decided that rather than analyzing the good works of others, he would be of greater use to God working with the poor in Mexico and focusing more on actually doing good works. In any event, Alanzo knew well the extent to which the very idea of a miracle could distort people's expectations. These things needed to be looked at very carefully.

"Maria," answered Alanzo, "the Church teaches that anything is possible if it's the will of God. That happens to be a teaching especially close to my heart. I have seen many things

The Mustard Seed

that I can only describe as wonders in my work with people over the years. But...," and he took a deep breath, "first, let Bernardo and me investigate this a little."

"She doesn't have much time, Alanzo."

Alanzo nodded with profound understanding, "Yes, it's very easy to get your hopes up. But then, if Theresa isn't healed...?"

Maria then saw Theresa standing in the hallway. Theresa looked up at Father Bernardo who was next to her and wiped away a tear. Then she smiled and entered the living room with her new balero.

"Look, Father Bernardo bought me a new balero," said Theresa.

Maria stood and picked Theresa up in her arms. "Well, let's go in your room and you can show me how to use it."

"Okay," said Theresa. "Can I sleep with you tonight?"

"Of course." Maria walked her daughter into the bedroom as Theresa waved good-night to her uncle and Father Bernardo.

Bernardo said to Alanzo, "Did I hear you say something about us investigating something?"

Fathers Bernardo and Alanzo had first become friends when they were both working for the Congregation for the Causes of the Saints. Bernardo had, by his own admission, become somewhat jaded by that experience until one day he said to his confessor, "I feel that all this emphasis on the need for wonders and miracles may foster more religiosity than it does true faith." His father confessor was surprisingly supportive and urged him to continue to pray for guidance. It was about that time that, through the beautiful serendipity that people of faith identify as the guidance of God, Bernardo found that he and Alanzo had been reassigned to a developing ministry in Mexico. So he had left the miracle-hunting business but had since found, to his surprise, that in directly helping those in need, he would encounter even more miracles, not fewer.

"On the news just now," replied Alanzo, "there was a story about a little girl who lives around here. Supposedly she has seen Jesus and she healed a crippled boy."

"Well," said Bernardo, "I've always felt that Jesus has a special relationship with children."

In Theresa's bedroom she was lying in bed, snuggling next to her mother. Theresa asked, "What did you see on TV that you were talking to Uncle Alanzo about?"

Maria could see a glint of hope in Theresa's eyes. Maria found herself thinking, "What is life without hope?"

Meanwhile Alanzo and Bernardo continued to ponder.

"So what are you saying?" Alanzo asked. "We should maybe--?"

"I'm thinking perhaps we should look into this."

"No, you're right. Let's find this news lady and maybe find out where this little girl attends church."

CHAPTER 11

The "news lady," Dolores Clark, of course, knew not only where the little girl attended church, but a whole lot more. After all, Dolores was not merely a probing journalist. She had grown up in White Dove and still lived there, at least some of the time, whenever her TV news career two hours away in L.A. would allow it. And like most people in the village, she had always instinctively made a point of knowing as much as possible about everyone she knew. And yes, she did know just about everyone, including and especially Bonnie Hopkins, whom Dolores remembered as Bonnie Donovan when they were on the cheerleading squad together at Theodore Roosevelt High School. Bonnie was always the pretty one and got most of the attention, while Dolores – well, she was ambitious and hard-working – and cute in a girl-next-door way. In freshman year she hated Bonnie for her looks and social ease. But by graduation they were friends. That's how Bonnie was. How can you hate somebody who treats everyone so nice? And of course, Dolores found her own way, graduating from U.C. Berkeley with a degree in journalism.

As she drove back to the TV station in Hollywood that night to get ready for the eleven o'clock broadcast, Dolores was high as a kite, looking forward to what a hero she would be after that killer segment she did on Sara. Surprises are what make the news and she certainly found one when she got to her office.

"Dolores! I need you in here!" The shout across the newsroom was from the office of her fast-talking Executive Producer, Jacob Colson. He was a slightly pudgy fifty-one, but seemed older as he sat behind his desk, popping Pepcids with his coffee. Not a good sign.

She stepped into his office. "Yes, Boss?"

He began with an arched look: "'The Miracles of Sara Hopkins'? Really?"

"Yes, really. What was wrong with it?"

"'What was wrong with it,'" Jacob said as he ran his fingers through his thinning hair, "is that I got a call from network immediately after your segment ran. And not just anybody; Bob Warman himself called -- the head of network news -- asking if I'm a shill for some kind of Christians-in-broadcasting kind of movement."

"You're kidding."

"Do I look like I'm kidding?!"

"I was reporting the facts."

"Facts, schmacts! Dolores, honey, this ain't journalism school. Have you been paying attention? Do you understand what we do here?"

"I think I do."

"Let me refresh you," said Jacob. "We've got a whole lot of people we've gotta make nice to. Like there's a wide-based audience with all kinds of beliefs and non-beliefs, and there's sponsors and there's,... you know, I mean, uh – oh, hell, let's just call them Watchdogs. Okay? You understand what I'm saying?"

"Go on."

"We have to be 'fair and balanced.'"

"But I am – "

"Shut up! I'm not through ranting! You know what 'fair and balanced' means? Never mind. I'll tell you what it means. It means when you've a got a story that's, like, something weird, something with religious overtones, something science can't explain, you don't step out in front of it and call it a 'miracle.' No! You call it 'a mystery.' You use phrases like, 'alleged cures' and 'she claims she saw Jesus.' You see the difference? You can't act like you actually believe in this stuff or our credibility as a news show will be out the window. Hey, you can't even act like you actually know anything."

"But what if it's real?" said Dolores.

"No, what if you just think it's real?" said Jacob. "I know you think you can read these people because it's like your hometown, right? I mean I know you're from up there in, uh, Pigeon Hollow -- "

"White Dove!"

"Yeah, whatever. Anyway, you're undercutting your objectivity when you say you go to church with these kids. And most importantly, you cannot bite the hand that feeds you."

"'Bite the hand'? What?"

"Do I have to draw you a picture? Have you noticed who our sponsors are?"

Dolores shrugged, beyond stunned. When Jacob got on a roll like this, she had learned to just step out of his way until his steam was gone.

"Half of them are big pharmaceuticals," Jacob went on. "They are not in the business of telling people they can be cured of disease by some damn religious superstition."

Dolores was an articulate, highly educated reporter, but she found herself virtually speechless. All she could muster was, "Wow."

"Wow, indeed," said Jacob. "Now tomorrow, for the follow up on this, I'd think in terms of maybe an interview with, I don't know, some nice, agnostic medical doctor, or maybe a professor of some sort, who can talk about the issue from the other side."

"'The other side'?"

"Fair and balanced!" said Jacob as he rose, grabbing his jacket. "Now get out of here, I have a meeting upstairs."

CHAPTER 12

As Father Alanzo Echevarria lay in bed that night, he found himself, to his own surprise, fascinated, in fact virtually seized, by vivid imaginings of what Sara Hopkins might be capable of. If only the TV reports were anywhere near true....

He had come up to White Dove from his parish in Michoacan for a vacation, to relax a little. That's what he had told Theresa. Actually, as Maria knew all too well, he had come because these next few weeks figured to be the last time he'd get to see his niece alive. Her prognosis was not good. This little girl, this Sara, held out more hope for Theresa than anything else that had crossed his path. True, most people may not see it that way, but then Alanzo had a special affinity for the miraculous. Of course, he had nearly overdosed on the subject during his stint as an official investigator, but this case felt very new and at once curiously fresh and familiar. As Alanzo's head hit the pillow he was suddenly overcome with a wave of pure relaxation and fell immediately into a dream. It was a dream he had had before, many, many times. It was in fact the very dream that had set him off on a course which would last him throughout his life, inquiring about the nature of unexplained wonders and the nature of God himself. This when he was eight-years-old.

In the dream, which was always the same, a seven-year-old Alanzo, dressed in his navy-blue, First Holy Communion suit with a white bow tie, enters the main doors of the 16th Century Church of St. Peter in his home-town of Limpias, Spain. He stops in the vestibule, puts two fingers of his right hand in the holy water font and blesses himself with the sign of the cross.

As he enters the center aisle of the nave, he stops and genuflects. Then slowly, reverently, he walks the entire length of the richly decorated baroque church toward the high altar, above which hangs the magnificent 17th Century crucifix sculpted by Pedro de Mena. The boy, looking up all around him, is overwhelmed by the size and beauty of the church, the frescoes, the gold-framed figures. Then as he reaches the sanctuary, little Alanzo gets on both knees and stares up wide-eyed at the crucifix. De Mena, one of the greatest religious sculptors of the Spanish Baroque, was known for his dramatic and realistic portrayals, and this crucifix was maybe his finest work. Jesus on the cross is life-sized, nearly two meters tall, feet and hands pierced by nails, blood pouring onto his brow from the crown of thorns, the flesh torn and bruised and with the most life-like eyes ever seen in a statue, looking up toward heaven. This is a meditation on the sufferings of the Savior in the final moments of his agony. The effect is one that is at once horrific and yet exquisitely beautiful, leaving the viewer profoundly moved. And in the dream, as little Alanzo kneels, he closes his eyes and prays:

"Lord, I am not worthy of your sacrifice, I ask only that you show me how I may serve you."

When he opens his eyes, he is startled to see the Crucified One has closed his eyes. Looking all the harder, Little Alanzo sees the eyes now slowly open and gaze directly upon him. The little boy is amazed and stares open-mouthed at the figure. Then he hears, softly, but somehow reverberating throughout the church, his name, "Alanzo," being spoken by the Crucified Christ.

Astonished, he replies, "Yes, My Lord?"

"Trust," says the Christ.

"Trust?"

"Trust in the visions of the faithful," comes the Voice very slowly, firmly, gently. "Even as you trust in your faith. Your faith in me."

Little Alanzo stares wide-eyed. He has no idea what this means. Then the figure returns to its original pose and appearance, eyes cast heavenward. As the astounded little boy watches, he is tapped on the shoulder. He looks up to see a priest whom he recognizes from the family pictures as his great-great uncle, Thomas Echevarria, the pastor of this church.

"Come, get up now, son; it's time to go."

Little Alanzo obediently rises and slowly walks back up the aisle alongside the black-cassocked figure.

"You have to go back," says Father Thomas as they walk. "This is only 1919 and you haven't been born yet. You have to wait your turn."

"Then why am I here, Father?"

"Because some day you will spread the secret of this miracle to others and it will be a blessing to the world."

"Good Father Thomas, I don't understand. What is the secret of this miracle?"

Father Thomas smiles down at the Little Alanzo: "Go back. Go back." And he fades away, as does the Church of St. Peter. That's how the dream always ended and this time was no exception, only when the grown-up Father Alanzo awakened this time, he found himself especially wound up, sweating on his pillow and anxious for his little niece in the next room.

CHAPTER 13

Early the next morning outside the Hopkins house, three-dozen cars were parked along the street up and down the block. Parents stood with their crippled and sick children in the front yard. Some of the children were in wheel chairs, others stood on crutches. There was a little blind girl who wore dark glasses and carried a cane and held her mother's hand. And then there was little Theresa, a kerchief over her chemo-depilated head, holding Maria's hand. Standing behind them were Father Alanzo and Father Bernardo, wearing their Roman clerical collars. The parents stood next to their children with hope in their eyes and prayers in their hearts.

Inside the Hopkins house, Danny was freaked out as he peeked through the blinds of the front room. "Dad! These people all want to see Sara!"

Alex and Bonnie looked out and Alex said, "Danny, I'm afraid you're right."

"Oh, my God," said Bonnie, "what are we going to do?"

"I'll go out there," said Alex, "and ask them to leave."

"You can't, Dad," came Sara's voice from behind them.

They turned to see Sara, standing there in her yellow bathrobe. "What if I was sick," she said, "and there was a possibility that you could do something to help me?"

"Sara, darling," said Bonnie, "you said it wasn't you who healed Mark. You said it was his faith in Jesus. What if these children don't have that faith?"

"But what if they do?"

Bonnie was exasperated, very afraid for her little girl: "What if it's not God's plan that they should be healed?"

"God's plan?" Sara thought, "Wasn't that his business?" But Sara said nothing. She just shrugged.

Alex went to one knee and put an arm around her. "You're just a little girl, Sara," he said. "If you go out there and they are healed, I'm afraid you'll never have a chance to be that little girl again."

"Your father's right," said Bonnie. "More and more people will come. It'll never stop."

Meanwhile, Danny, without saying anything to anyone, opened the front door and stepped outside. There was a stir in the crowd as Danny stood on the front porch, pulled out his comb and began to comb his hair. Then he waved at everyone. The crowd just gawked at him and he gave them a big smile, then suddenly they stopped buzzing and focused sharply: Sara had stepped out onto the porch behind him and just stood there silently in her bright yellow bathrobe, looking like a diminutive ball of sunlight. All the people suddenly fell still. It was a strangely anti-climactic moment.

Theresa felt a little disappointed. She looked up at her mother. "She's just a little girl like me. I've seen her at school."

She took Maria's hand and started to lead her away, just as many of the kids who had gathered there started to turn and leave. But Theresa stopped and noticed that the two priests never moved; they just stood and stared at Sara. "Why?" Theresa wondered.

As the exodus began to grow, Sara suddenly piped up and said, "Wait, stop!" She focused in on Theresa, who had stopped and was looking at Sara, who then walked over to Theresa. "I did see Jesus," Sara told Theresa, "I don't know if I can help you. But I did see him. He brought a bird back to life. And he healed Mark Miller when Mark touched my hands."

Sara took Theresa's hand and held it for a few moments. Then Theresa let go of her hand and hugged her with a big, "Thank you!"

And then Sara walked over to the little blind girl and reached out and took her hands. Some moments passed until the little girl let go and took off her glasses. Then she seemed to squint for a moment in Sara's direction, hesitated, moved her head from side to side like a cat looking into a bright light, and she started to describe Sara to a T: "You have blonde hair," said the little girl, apparently no longer so blind, "your eyes are blue and you are very pretty."

"You can see her?" said her mother. "You can see?! Oh, my God, you can see!" The mother fell to her knees in astonished excitement and sheer, overwhelming joy as her daughter hugged Sara. A major buzz went through the crowd.

Two more mothers walked their daughters over to Sara as Theresa intently watched all of it while standing next to her mother, Maria, and the two priests. That's when Theresa almost had to pinch herself when she found herself realizing that she was seeing a figure that she took to be Jesus, bathed in a soft, white light, standing next to Sara and placing his hand on Sara's shoulder as she touched one child after another. Theresa was utterly stunned by this vision and stared at Sara and Jesus for several moments, totally rapt. It never occurred to Theresa to speak of the apparition to anyone, it seemed such a personal revelation in her heart. And although she had no idea what it meant, Theresa could feel that this was more than a passing image outside of her, rather it seemed to penetrate to some deep, hidden part of her mind and body. She only knew for sure that it felt very good. Finally, she just turned to Maria and said quietly, "I think I'm going to be okay, Mom."

Father Alanzo, of course, like most of the others, saw only Sara and the kids touching her. He watched as a twelve-year-old boy wearing a Clippers jersey rolled up in a wheelchair and touched Sara's hand, as if in slow-motion. Then the boy stood up, and suddenly Sara fell to the ground as if struck. The mothers and children around her were startled nearly out of their skins. They closed in around her and reached out, but Sara lay stone-cold still with eyes closed in some sudden and very private sleep.

Alanzo and Bernardo were on her in a heartbeat as Alex came racing out of the house and picked her up in his arms. Maria, too, rushed over to them.

"Is she okay?" asked Father Alanzo.

"I don't know," said Alex. How indeed would he know? He had already been afraid for her, but now this? Utterly panicked, he picked Sara up and hurriedly carried her into the house.

Meanwhile, Theresa squeezed her mother's hand while the two priests were both agape: they saw the "blind girl" tracking Alex with her eyes and the Lakers boy who had been in the wheelchair now standing next to his mother.

"The children," said Father Alanzo, "look at them!"

Bernardo and Alanzo shared a look of both amazement and recognition. The entire crowd was abuzz with what surely appeared to be at least two more miracles.

CHAPTER 14

Sara was awake but woozy. "How do you feel now, Sara?" Alex asked. They sat along with Bonnie and Danny in Dr. Riley's office.

"Same as before," said Sara. "My head hurts and I feel weak and tired."

Dr. Riley entered. "We've done all her blood work. I've called the hospital and I've scheduled her for an MRI. They'll be waiting for you."

"She was sick after she prayed for the bird," said Bonnie, "then same thing after praying for Mark Miller. Now look at her. She's exhausted. What do you think is wrong with her?"

"I can't say yet," said the Doctor. "Let's wait until all the test results are in and see what we find."

"You weren't there, Doctor," Bonnie continued. "A kid in a wheelchair got up and walked. A blind girl could see again. What's going on? How can any of this be happening?"

"I don't know," said Dr. Riley. "And we don't know the history of those children. Let's first find out what's wrong with your daughter. Then we can figure out what happened in your front yard."

Then Nurse Anna put her head in the door: "Doctor, I think you and the Hopkins' should come to the waiting room. I think you need to see this."

As everyone regrouped in the waiting room, what they found was a gathering of some half-dozen folks crowded around the TV as reporter Dolores Clark was on the television, broadcasting live from in front of the Hopkins home. Dolores had planned a careful, back-pedaling, know-nothing kind of report, as per Jacob Colson's orders. But what she witnessed in the Hopkins front yard had so startled her that, at the last minute, she decided to blow off her boss's instructions and go with her heart and with the truth as she saw it.

"Just hours ago, on the spot where I am standing now, miracles were performed. A little blind girl can now see. A crippled boy can walk. And a little girl with cancer may have been healed. The miracle worker seems to be our own little Sara Hopkins who gets visits from Jesus."

As the broadcast continued, Dr. Riley looked out the window and said, "They're not here yet, but I think we'd better get Sara out of here."

Alex agreed. "I don't want Sara interviewed on TV. It will just draw more and more people."

"I know," said Dr. Riley. "This is becoming exactly what I was afraid of."

Meanwhile, in front of the Hopkins home, Fathers Echevarria and Moretti watched from the crowd on the sidelines as Dolores wrapped her stand-up: "...reporting live from White Dove, this is Dolores Clark, Channel 14 news."

As the crowd began to disperse and Dolores folded her notes and made her way back to the microwave truck, the priests approached her. "Excuse me, Ms. Clark," said Father Echevarria, "could we have a minute?"

Well, as it turned out she gave them more than a minute. An hour later, the priests barely remembered to touch their cappuccinos as they sat on the edge of their seats in Jeff's Coffee Emporium on White Dove Avenue in rapt attention to Dolores's tales of Sara Hopkins. They found that Dolores knew not only Bonnie Hopkins but her daughter, as well, and not just because she went to church with her.

"There's not much that goes unnoticed in a small town, especially if you live here long enough," said Dolores. "Now, I'm not going to tell you that this miracle business didn't come as a surprise to me, but I've always known that little Sara had something really special about her. She was always generous with the other kids; I never saw her get into a fight, but there was one thing I did see that was about the bravest thing I'd ever seen a young child do."

"Bravest?" asked Father Moretti.

"Absolutely. When I first moved back to town here about three years ago, I rented a house that was four doors down from where the Hopkins live. Now most of the time I was working, so I wasn't home that much and was too busy to really get to know everyone on my street. But Bonnie I knew from high school and I got used to seeing Sara playing with the other kids on the street. She was like five-years-old at the time and I didn't pay much attention to her. All I knew was that she seemed very popular; all the other kids liked her. Well it happened one day that I was at home and I had my leg in a cast because I was recovering from knee surgery. But I was going stir-crazy in the house so I hobbled out to the front yard and started pruning my roses; I like working with flowers; it relaxes me. And suddenly I heard from just down the street a little boy yelling, 'Don't do that! You're going to hurt yourself. Come back down!' I looked up and saw this little blonde girl climbing up a gnarly old oak tree. And of course it was Sara and she was way high up there. I was shocked at the sheer altitude. I dropped my pruning shears and bounced on over, crutches and all, to where the little boy was standing looking up and I said, 'Sara, honey, come back down. That's dangerous.'

"And she said to me, over her shoulder, real casual-like, 'Yeah, I'm coming down. But first I've got to get Caruso.'

"'Get what?' I said.

"'Caruso.'

"'What's that?' Then I felt the little boy tug my pant leg and he pointed upward and off to the left. I looked and that's when I saw it: Caruso was a dark brown, fluffy little cat, I thought maybe a Tabby or a Maine Coon, perched high up on what looked like a precariously thin branch. Well, of course, my heart sank as I was certain there was no way this was going to end well for this little girl if she didn't just back down immediately.

"My first thought was I have to climb up there and bring her down. Then like half a second later I realized that was a non-starter. With my cast I couldn't even bend my knee, let alone climb a tree and even if I got up there, I probably couldn't carry her down without killing us both. So I said to the little boy, 'Timmy, go, run and get Mrs. Hopkins! Hurry!' So he ran off. Meanwhile, I was watching Sara and she was coming to thinner and thinner branches.

"'Sara, sweetie,' I yelled up to her, 'you've got me really worried. Come back down and we'll get the fire department to rescue the cat.'

"'No,' she said, 'they'll scare Caruso.'"

"'Honey,' I said, 'you're scaring the daylights out of me right now.'"

"And you know what she did? She just laughed and said, 'Don't worry, Miss Clark, it's not my time to go.'"

"'You don't know that!' I said.

"'Yes, I do,' she said, and she was giggling. Five years-old she was!"

The priests looked at each other.

"And then, get this: the branch she's on starts to crack, and as the branch gives way, she grabs onto another branch, but her feet are still dangling in the air! Like forty feet up! I was sure she was going to come crashing down. But, no, she somehow pulls herself up, gets a leg up over the branch and next thing I know, she climbs even higher – just about on a level with where the cat is. Now she was really just swinging in the wind. And this is where I was really very worried about her because I knew she was going to go for the cat, but to get there, she would have to hang on to some super-thin branches. Well, Sara sits on that high branch, still about six feet away from the cat, and she calls out to the cat: 'Caruso, come to me.' Now I was even more worried, because I remember thinking that certainly won't work. Everybody knows that when a cat climbs a tree like this, it's freaked out and shies away from contact. So I figured Sara would have to risk herself even more to go out and get her."

Dolores stopped shook her head and took a deep breath.

"So what happened?" asked a rapt Father Moretti.

Dolores continued: "The cat slowly stood up on his branch and casually started to groom himself, you know, licking his own back and so on. And I was just praying that Sara would not try to get closer to the cat; the branches were just too thin.

"She calls out again, 'Caruso, sweetie, come to me now. Mrs. Grayson needs you to come home.'

"Suddenly the cat turns around and strolls slowly along the branch toward Sara, gets to her, rubs up against her, purrs and then leaps up to her and lands in the crook of her arm. If I hadn't seen it, I wouldn't have believed it. So now she has the cat and the cat is purring away like he's at home in his bed.

"Right about then, Bonnie, her mother, comes running up, completely freaked out, and screams, 'Sara Hopkins, get down from there right now!'

"Well, Sara has always obeyed her mother and she goes, 'Yes, Mommy,' and starts climbing down. Meanwhile, Mrs. Grayson shows up, all in a sweat; she's the widow that lives across the street and now I just put it together: this Caruso is her cat, in fact the one that used to be the favorite pet of her late husband. I think Sara knew that Caruso was really important to Mrs. Grayson, and she wasn't doing so well; she'd had a stroke a while back.

"Anyway Mrs. Grayson is looking up and going, 'Oh my God, Sara, be careful!'

"'I'm okay, Mrs. Grayson. Look I've got Caruso!'

"'Honey, just get yourself down in one piece,' says Mrs. Grayson. 'Caruso can take care of himself. Bonnie, if anything happened to that child, I believe I'd just die on the spot.'

"And the widow carried on like that and Sara got to the ground safely, put Caruso in the widow's arms and Bonnie, of course, says something like, 'Sara you could have fallen!'

"And the little girl's comeback? 'Yes, Mommy, if I fell down and died I would just go to heaven and be with Jesus. So you don't need to worry.'"

The priests were flabbergasted.

"You see what I mean about this kid?"

The priests just stared at her, speechless.

CHAPTER 15

Alex and Bonnie looked out the Doctor's window and saw three micro-wave trucks from different TV stations pulling up in front of the medical office.

Dr. Riley pulled the Hopkins' back into his office, out of earshot of the others in the waiting room. "After you get the tests done at the hospital, is there anywhere you can go other than home?"

"We can go to my dad's ranch," said Bonnie.

"Okay," said Dr. Riley. "Let's you and I go get Sara. Alex, why don't you go get the car and pull it around to the back of the office?"

"Alright," said Alex. "Danny, come with me."

As Danny followed Alex he said, "I want to be on TV." "Good," said Alex, "we'll put you in a box and ship you to the TV station."

"No!"

As the Doctor and Bonnie walked quickly to the examination room, he said, "Sara said she saw Jesus in her front yard while the children were there. Did you see him?"

"I don't know what's going on with that," said Bonnie. "But crippled kids got up and walked and a blind girl said she could see. That much I know."

Now, Dr. Riley had been raised in a deeply spiritual tradition. His father, Al, had been a good friend of Pastor Bob, Sr., even as

David had grown up close to Bob, Jr., and together they had been raised to believe in the power of prayer. But over time, between the years at Stanford and medical school in San Francisco, he had acquired a different perspective. And adversity had taught him some other lessons. Now, faced with these strange goings on, Dr. David Riley was dumbfounded. On the one hand he clung to the materialist path in which he had been trained – the doctrine that insisted that no matter the apparent result, there was officially "no evidence" for the reality of miracles. At the same time, part of him flashed on an inkling of the idea that the very tenacity of his clinging to scientific dogma was bolstered by a secret fear of yet another disappointment at the altar of faith. And yet he sensed his grip being incrementally loosened, whether he wanted to or not.

In the examination room, Anna removed a thermometer from Sara's mouth. "For what it's worth, she does not have a temperature," said Anna, "but she is off the chart on the sweetness meter."

That made Sara smile.

The Doctor said, "Sara your mother is going to take you to the hospital for a few more tests."

"After the tests, will I get to go home?"

"We're going to go stay over at Grandpa's for a few days," said Bonnie.

"Oh, good! I like that."

So Bonnie got Sara dressed and left through the back door to the alley, where Alex waited in the blue Ford Explorer and they drove off with nary a soul the wiser.

Dr. Riley, meanwhile, stepped out the front door and fielded the onslaught of media cameras and microphones and repetitive questions, stonewalling all the way on the inevitable inquiries about miracles: "... it's way too early... we are still gathering the medical data... I cannot comment on any questions regarding anything like miracles..." etc., etc.

At the hospital later, after Sara's MRI was complete, Dolores Clark's micro-wave truck pulled into the parking lot, followed by five other news trucks -- just after the Hopkins' Explorer pulled out and escaped down the highway into the night, heading for El Rancho de la Paloma Blanca.

Sam stepped out onto his porch as the Hopkins' car pulled up to the ranch house. He went over, opened the back door and picked up Sara in his arms.

"How's my beautiful little girl?"

"I'm good."

Danny got out of the car and began combing his hair. "Am I beautiful, too, Grandpa?"

Sam and Sara just laughed.

"No!" said Sara. Danny looked a little shocked. "But you're handsome," she continued.

"Everybody get in the house," said Sam. "I've made us some dinner."

"Dad, you didn't have to do that," said Bonnie

"Didn't want these kids to starve. How does spaghetti with basil, tomatoes and garlic in olive oil sound?"

"Sounds good to me," said Sara.

"What about dessert?" said Danny.

"I made Tiramisu," said Sam.

Danny wrinkled his nose. "What's that?"

"I think you'll like it," said Sam.

"What if I don't like it?"

"I hope you don't," said Alex, "because I'm going to eat yours."

"No way, it's mine," said Danny.

And so the family filed into the house with Sam carrying Sara. The dinner that followed was the kind that Bonnie had fond memories of from her youth. Sam had always enjoyed cooking; he had learned most of what he knew from Bonnie's mother. He grew most of his own vegetables and his herb garden was always in bloom. His zest for the life that he had shared with Rachel came through in the bold dishes that he favored, as did the love with which he made them. For Bonnie these flavors seemed to bring her mother back again in a small way and it made her happy. The adults complemented the pasta with a velvety local Zinfandel made by one of Sam's neighbors. And then it was time for dessert.

"I have two favorite desserts," said Sara. "Tiramisu and Crostata di Frutta."

"I didn't know that," said Sam.

"Yes, you did," Sara laughed. "You know I love both of them."

"That must be why I made them both."

"You did?!"

"I want chocolate cake," said Danny.

"Be glad you're getting what you're getting," said Bonnie.

"We also have chocolate cake," said Sam.

"Dad, you're crazy."

And so the evening went. Bonnie and Alex found themselves relieved and grateful for the simple but excellent meal, a glass of warming red wine, Sam's good company and a short respite from the day. It had been a hard one and it wouldn't be over yet. As Alex played Nintendo with Sara and Danny in the den, Sam spoke quietly with Bonnie in the front room.

"So what did the doctor say?"

Bonnie shrugged. "He's supposed to call me after he looks at the tests."

"When will that be?"

As if on cue, Bonnie's cell phone rang. "Maybe right now," she said. As Bonnie answered and strolled into the other room to talk, Sam found his gaze turned for the moment to the den, where his grandchildren and Alex were intently playing Nintendo. Looking at them brought a smile to his face and he counted himself a lucky man not only for the having of his family but for knowing the pure joy of his own deep and unshakeable love for them. Sam found himself grateful beyond all imagination to be in the presence of such simple beauty and love as now was his, especially because he remembered a time when all of that seemed beyond his grasp.

He had been a soldier in his youth. The war in Vietnam was hugely unpopular among his age group, but growing up on the ranch, he had paid little attention to the protest movements.

Instead he volunteered for the Army because he saw it as an opportunity – a chance to leave White Dove and see the world – and to harness the raging fire in his belly. Special Forces – that was what called out to him. As a Green Beret, he wasn't just a good soldier, he was fearsome one. The young Sam Donovan loved what he did and was as dangerous a man as ever wore an American uniform -- until he had more than his fill and learned that he didn't want to do it any more. In his heart, he was a protector. That's what Sam was always about. And now, looking at these young people on his living room floor, he wanted to throw his arms around them and keep this moment forever safe, against all reason, from the harm he knew the world might bring.

When Bonnie returned, her short conversation with the doctor being over, she hung up the phone and as she stood in the hallway, leaning with one hand against the doorjamb, her ashen face told Sam the story. The details of the story, as Bonnie haltingly gave out, were that Sara apparently had a brain tumor. The test data had been sent out to a specialist. Dr. Riley didn't want to give any opinion until after he talked to the specialist.

Sam didn't want to believe it. "When will he --?"

"Tomorrow," she said. "We probably won't know anything until tomorrow."

"This doesn't make sense," said Sam. "With all those kids she's been healing, it just doesn't make sense."

Bonnie took a deep breath and said, "I'm going to see if she and Danny want to go get some ice cream."

"There's some in the refrigerator."

But that wasn't what Bonnie had in mind. "I just want to take them some place and spend time with them," she said.

Sam nodded his understanding. "I'll be here when you get back."

Back in town, Pastor Jenkins' wife, Lucy, wondered who could be ringing the doorbell of the rectory at this hour. It was almost nine o'clock; a late hour for company in White Dove.

She opened the door to find two priests. They wanted to see Pastor Jenkins. No problem, said Lucy, but they would have to wait until he finished what seemed to her to be an exasperating phone call with Dr. Riley.

Finally, the Pastor hung up and Lucy stuck her head into his office: "Bob, there is a Father Echevarria and a Father Moretti who would like to speak with you."

"Of course, show them in."

The priests entered and shook the Pastor's hand. "Pastor Jenkins, I'm Father Echevarria and this is Father Moretti. He's from Rome. He was helping me in my Parish in Mexico but right now we are here visiting my sister-in-law whose daughter has cancer. That is, she had cancer until a little girl in your town apparently healed her. We have no conclusive medical proof yet, but her symptoms have cleared up dramatically within a few hours."

"Ah, yes," said Pastor Jenkins.

"I understand that you know Sara Hopkins?"

"Since before she was born." The Pastor rose and motioned his guests toward two leather chairs. "Please."

The priests sat and the Pastor continued: "So your niece was one of the children who was healed?"

"Yes," said Father Echevarria, "she had stage-four cancer and now...well, there's no sign of it. We witnessed this event ourselves."

"You know," said Pastor Jenkins, "I would like to believe that these are truly miracles."

"And so would we. That's why we're here. Could you possibly tell us about Sara?"

The Pastor leaned back and nodded.

Meanwhile, at an outside table in front of the Dairy Queen off the highway, just over the White Dove city limits, Alex and Bonnie enjoyed ice cream sundaes with Sara and Danny.

Danny said to Sara, "Mine's really, really good. How does yours taste?"

Sara was really focused on her sundae. "Mine's good."

"I have chocolate M&M'S, bananas, and whipped cream," said Danny. "Do you want to taste it?"

"No."

"What's on yours?" asked Danny.

"Hot fudge with whipped cream and strawberries."

"That sounds really good," said Danny. "You can try some of mine if you want."

"No, thanks."

"I wonder what yours tastes like."

"The hot fudge is really good," she said.

"I wish I would have got some hot fudge."

Sara took another bite. "Mmm, it's really good, especially when you eat the strawberries and the hot fudge at the same time."

"You sure you don't want to taste mine?"

"No, mine's so good I don't want to eat anything else."

Danny by now couldn't even believe it. He just kept on plugging. She has to get the hint sometime, right?

"I bet it's really good." he said.

"Next time," Sara said, "you'll have to order this. It's the best."

Danny just couldn't stop staring at her as she enjoyed every bite. Then suddenly, she stopped eating, sat up straight and looked down at her bowl, still half full of ice cream, hot fudge and juicy strawberries. Danny arched a little: was this his chance? Well, it turned out no, as Sarah impulsively swept her whole container into the trash can next to the table.

Danny couldn't believe it. "But, but, but, but...." He sounded like a small motorboat. "Why did you throw it away?"

"I didn't want any more," said Sara.

"But I wanted to taste it."

"Why didn't you ask?"

"I thought I did," Danny said weakly. Finally, he just shook his head and gave up.

Bonnie leaned over and asked the kids, "Do you want anything else?"

"No," said Sara, "I'm full."

"I want what Sara had," said Danny.

"Eat your sundae first," said Bonnie, "and we'll talk about it."

Danny gave her a look that said, "You're kidding?"

Bonnie then put her arm around Sara. "Dr. Riley called."

"What did he say?"

Bonnie hesitated inadvertently. She'd rather walk barefoot over burning coals than have this conversation. Sara felt her reticence. Bonnie looked like she might break into tears.

"They found something on the tests," said Bonnie. Alex took her hand under the table and she steadied.

Sara held onto her mother's arm, looked up at her and said, "I'll be okay, Mommy, as long as I know you're okay."

"I know, sweetheart. I just —"

"It'll be okay, Mommy. Really."

Bonnie and Alex share a look that only a parent could ever know, each feeling the exquisitely painful awareness that this, their precious little child, was concerned more with the well-being of her parents than with the possibility of her own untimely end. And this just made them need to weep all the more, but neither dared show it, lest they betray the strength that their roles demanded.

Alex said, "Does anyone want anything else before we go back to Grandpa's?"

"I want what Sara had."

"Your mother told you that you have to eat what you have first."

"Okay," said Danny, "then I don't want anything." He ate another spoonful of his sundae and moved over to his mother and Sara and gave them a hug.

As Fathers Echevarria and Moretti sat in Pastor Jenkins' study, they were an utterly rapt audience for his stories about Sara Hopkins. The priests didn't advertise to the Pastor their previous commission, investigating claims of sainthood, but already, they began to feel this young child seemed to show at least some of the earmarks of the right stuff, not only because of the miracles, but more importantly, because of the quality of her life.

"You know," said Pastor Jenkins, "if I think back to the whole time I've known her, and that of course is her entire life, I have to say, I've never met another little girl or for that matter any other person -- child or adult -- who was more kind or more simply devoted to God than she is."

"Would you call her a saint?" asked Father Moretti.

The Pastor hesitated. "Well, I understand that in the Catholic tradition the veneration of 'saints' is a big thing."

"That's true," smiled Father Echevarria. "It's something we encourage to the extent that it leads people closer to God."

Pastor Jenkins nodded, "I understand. Now, in our tradition, we don't do that so much. We try to acknowledge people who have lived a good life. We don't really focus on 'saints,' as such. But, that said, in my opinion, if ever there was a little girl who deserved to be called a saint, it's Sara Hopkins."

The priests shared a knowing look. But now the Pastor paused a moment and seemed a little flustered. "You know, I just realized, I'm being a terrible host. Would you care for some refreshment? A drink perhaps? Brandy? Coffee?"

The priests politely declined and then Pastor Jenkins bit his lip and spoke slowly and deliberately. "There is one other thing you should know. And what I am about to say, I tell you in confidence. I just got off the phone with Sara's doctor. Sara is very ill. She has a brain tumor. Fairly large. And it seems to be inoperable. The Doctor doesn't think she has more than two weeks to live."

The blood drained from the priests' suddenly very pale faces as they realized there was indeed a lot going on here.

"It doesn't really make sense, does it?" Pastor Jenkins continued, "All these people she's been healing, and yet... I just hope people don't take this as some sort of... I don't know, as some sort of dark and negative sign... You know what I mean?"

And as the priests looked at each other, they both knew exactly what the Pastor meant, because they were both thinking the same thing: there was something here that was oddly and painfully familiar to them.

CHAPTER 16

Fathers Echevarria and Moretti found themselves hearkening back to what became their final assignment for the Congregation for the Causes of the Saints. It was late one October that they had arrived for the first time in the town of Patzcuaro in the Mexican state of Michoacan. They came there, to this beautiful, rustic, cobble-stoned, 16th Century colonial city to investigate the case of one Socorro Ramon, a local woman who had died some ten years earlier, and who was reputed to have been a great healer during her life. She was believed to have caused many healings and miracles after her passing.

Father Alvaro De La Valle was the pastor of the parish that Socorro had attended. He had known her well and was full of information about her. As the two visiting priests sat in the old pastor's rectory, they spent days conversing with him as well as going through the voluminous files he had accumulated. They were able to form a detailed picture of this woman's life. The youngest daughter of a Tarascan Indian peasant family, Socorro had spent her early childhood alongside her parents and siblings in the corn and strawberry fields and avocado orchards, tending whatever crops were in season. Even as a child, she was known to have a healing touch and would relieve the aches and pains and injuries of her family and their neighbors and co-workers. Oddly enough, at first, while this made her mildly popular, no one made much of it. As Father De La Valle explained, these were poor people, close to the earth. Many had never been to a real doctor and relying on folk medicine was a tradition they were used to, going back to the days before the Spanish. So when she would lay her hands on people and they felt better, no one was shocked. They accepted it as something she had a gift for. It seemed normal. At the same time, she was quietly but deeply spiritual and devoted to God. In her teens, to help her family get more money, she landed a job as a domestic in the home of a wealthy merchant in Patzcuaro. In time she married, had children, was widowed and carried on. All the while, her reputation for healing grew, and people would come to her from all the local villages. Although she would be exhausted from her job at the end of the day, she would never turn away anyone who needed her and there were many reports of healings that even the most jaded locals considered miraculous. The blind seeing, the lame walking, the diseased cured, etc. Through it all, Socorro remained humble. She took no credit, said the healings were caused by God, she but the instrument. And apart from the working of such "wonders," Socorro was constantly serving the poor in more conventional ways. As the two investigating priests discovered at the end of that October, Patzcuaro and the surrounding area have one of the most elaborate and best attended Day of the Dead celebrations in Mexico. For a whole week, the city and the lake area surrounding are decorated with flowers and there are crafts and arts competitions, music, dancing, and various food feasts, all connected with honoring the memory of those who have passed on. One event is called the "teruscan," in which children run around town gathering ears of corn, squash and chayotes from off of the neighbors' roofs, pretending to steal them. The "stolen" food is brought to the church community center to be cooked to feed the people.

"Socorro was always at the heart of these festivities," said Father De La Valle.

She was there to plan them, and run them and help cook the food and serve it to the community. Then she was the last to leave afterwards as she helped to clean up. And amazingly, after she passed, Socorro's fame grew. A large group of her friends and supporters, including some who never knew her in life, swore by the healing miracles she continued to generate after her death. A sort of cult had sprung up in her memory and they would pray to her for intercession with God and they would document the healings – which seemed to be not infrequent.

It was clear that Father De La Valle had great affection for Socorro and the two visitors were duly impressed. But Father Moretti couldn't help but notice that on the parish's archive shelf there was one bundled file docket that clearly had Socorro Ramon's name on it but Father De La Valle had not included it in their review documents.

And then Father Echevarria asked, "By the way, how did she die?"

Father De La Valle then grew very earnest. "She was struck suddenly by a cancer. What they call non-Hodgkins lymphoma. Within a few weeks she was gone."

"That must have been very sad for you," said Father Moretti.

"It was. I was with her at the end. But...," and then Father De La Valle struggled to find words, "it wasn't just losing her that was sad, it was some of what came afterwards."

"What came afterwards?"

"Some people in the community had trouble with her dying."

"Trouble...?" asked Father Moretti. The priests clearly found this puzzling. "How...?"

Socorro's old pastor gathered himself. This was a subject he loathed, but he needed to make sure these advocates of the Church heard it from him first. "Socorro spent her whole life healing others. It was something people came to expect of her. And always she gave the glory to God. But then, when this, this thing struck her down, there were some in the parish here who were horrified. More than that, they were disappointed. In her. As if it were her fault that while she could cure others, herself she would not save."

"So, some saw that as a problem?" asked Father Moretti

"They saw it as a curse," said Father De la Valle. "They said God had turned his back on her. And it made them rethink their ideas of her personal holiness. I do not share these opinions, you understand. But before you are through with your investigation, you will meet many people here who knew Socorro. And I want you to go and meet them, because the people who really knew her well all love her and they are passionate about supporting her for sainthood. But before you do, you will see this."

And he put the "hidden" folder on the table in front of them. "This is material that I am obliged to show you, even though in my personal opinion, these documents are at best misguided and vicious lies at worst."

The file, as the two Priests found, contained mostly letters, many of them anonymous, from people complaining to the Church about how Socorro was not really a saint but merely a talented hypnotist and trickster, or worse. While most people in town believed her to be a saint, the minority who protested her veneration were loud and occasionally abusive. They even shunned and publicly humiliated her siblings and her children. There were some eggings and some ugly graffiti.

When the Priests interviewed Socorro's daughter, Aliza Rodriguez, who had married a local tradesman who sold souvenirs to tourists, they were struck by her sweetness. She was not bitter about those who had turned on her mother and her family.

"They don't know any better. They're ignorant," said Aliza. "Some people even called her a bruja – a witch – getting her powers from the dark spirits." Aliza shook her head and smiled. "My mother was the most Christian woman I've ever known."

Father De la Valle agreed. "I knew Socorro Ramon since she was a child. I can tell you, she was as saintly a woman as ever walked the stones of these streets."

The report that Fathers Alanzo Echevarria and Bernardo Moretti wrote was a strong recommendation for beatification. But it didn't make her opposition go away. Now, five years later, her case was still pending – an object lesson in how radically people's vision can change if their saint shows any weakness.

And now, as Alanzo drove them back to Maria and Theresa's house, Bernardo turned to Alanzo. "So, do you think they're going to call Sara Hopkins a bruja?"

"You know, I am not really surprised at anything anymore. But let's see what happens. She's not dead yet."

CHAPTER 17

Old Butch was, not unlike Sam, a big guy and strong and in great shape for his age. He liked to lay his head on Sam's lap, especially when he thought Sam needed some cheering up. And this was surely one of those times, as Sam sat in the swing on his porch at one in the morning and stared out into the darkness, looking for shooting stars in the dark sky over the mountains. As he rubbed his old friend's big, blocky head, Sam found himself smiling at the wisdom and pure sweetness that seemed to come so naturally to dogs.

As Butch settled down to the floor and laid his head on top of Sam's boots, as was his habit when he was feeling protective, the front door opened and out came Sara, wrapped in a bathrobe over her pajamas. She came over to the swing and climbed up on Sam's lap.

"You can't sleep?" asked Sam.

She cuddled up to him and said, "Grandpa, I didn't want to say anything to Mommy, but I think she's afraid and I'm worried about her. I saw her holding Daddy and she was crying."

Sam nodded. "She's just a little worried about you."

"I know." Sara laid her head against Sam's chest and just sat there a moment. "Grandpa?"

"Yes?"

"I'm a little scared. Am I going to be okay?"

"You're going to be just fine."

"Mommy said I had a tumor on my brain. Is that dangerous?"

"It's dangerous," said Sam, "but you're going to be okay, Sara. I'm sure of it. We're going to get through this together. Okay?"

Sara rose up to his face and kissed his cheek. "Okay." She laid her head against his chest for a moment. Then she said, "Grandpa?"

"Yes?"

"How come everyone I touched got well and I got sick?"

"I'm not sure, honey," said Sam. Then as he reflected on the question, "It really doesn't make much sense though, does it?"

The next morning Sam decided to do something that made sense. He decided to go for a walk. Clear his head. And maybe, just maybe, find a bit of light. For Sara. And for himself at long last. And to do all that, he knew just where he had to go. Up the old dirt road through the woods, he went, along the short cut that led from the back of his property to White Dove Lake.

Bonnie had put on a larger pot of coffee than usual; she was expecting company. Pastor Jenkins and Dr. Riley didn't have to knock when they arrived. Bonnie opened the door and bade them wait in the front room.

"I'll get Alex," she said.

"Is Sara here?" asked the Pastor.

"I think it best if she isn't here when we talk," said Bonnie.

"Of course," said Dr. Riley.

Bonnie went to the den where Alex was playing Nintendo with Danny and Sara. "Sara," said Bonnie, "do you feel well enough to go play in the backyard with your brother for a while?"

"I feel well enough."

"Good. Is Grandpa still here?"

"No," said Sara, "he went for a walk and hasn't come back yet."

"Okay, well, I want you and your brother to go play on the swings until I call you."

"No, Mom," moaned Danny, "I want to play Nintendo."

Now Bonnie got serious. "Danny, you and Sara will go into the back yard and play until I call you. Okay?"

"Can we go bike riding?"

"Maybe later." Bonnie walked over to her two kids and took them in her arms and held them. "We'll go somewhere later. Somewhere fun. Okay?"

"To the rides?" asked Danny.

"The rides are kind of far away," said Bonnie. "Maybe the movies?"

"Or the video arcade?" said Danny.

"Sara, what do you want to do?" said Bonnie.

"Can we do both?"

"We might be able to do that."

"Okay," said Sara.

So the kids moved to the backyard while the adults sat down to coffee. Sara dutifully played on the swings, but she remained glum. Not her usual sunny self.

"Sara," asked Danny, "are you going to be okay?"

"I don't know. Mom was crying last night and I'm pretty sure the Doctor is here to talk about me. I wish I knew what he's saying," she said.

"We could sneak into the house and listen," said Danny.

"What if they catch us?"

"You can blame it on me."

"No, I wouldn't do that," she said.

"If we're real quiet, we won't get caught."

"If we do, I'll tell them it was my idea," she said.

"No," Danny said, "I don't want you to get in trouble."

"Okay, then let's not get caught."

That seemed to be a sensible plan for some reason, so they slipped off the swings and let them dangle in the breeze as they carefully approached the house.

Sam had approached his special spot by the lake with equal care, if not with stealth. He saw two red-tail hawks soar in the winds overhead, then looked across the misty lake and drank in the majesty of the place, as was his custom. And then he did something very different. Something he hadn't done in a long time. He began to pray.

"I know you can hear me," Sam whispered. "Figure you could have heard me back at the house. But I was thinking this place might be special, since Sara saw you here. So I figured right about now I could use all the help I could get, so I came here to say my piece."

Then he walked around some, a little awkward, like he was trying to figure what he should say. Praying was not something he had a lot of experience with. He picked up a flat rock and skimmed it across the glassy surface.

"I know I have no reason to think you would listen to me. Or show yourself to me. I have been very far from perfect. I know who I am and what I've done. I know I caused more than a little trouble when I was younger. Drank too much, fought all the time. Did things in Vietnam. And a few other places. And I know you know all that better than I do. I've got a lot to be sorry for.... Still, I did get married and I was a good husband. Went to work every day and raised a beautiful daughter. My wife always took her to church... even though I never went."

Sam walked closer to the water and looked around.

"I don't know exactly where my granddaughter was when she saw you. I just want you to know I would stand in that exact place if I could. You see, she's a beautiful child. She's way better than I ever was. She always loved you. Just believed in you right from the start. From the moment she first started talking she wanted to know everything she could about you. I could never tell her that much. The only thing I knew to tell her was she had to have faith in you and to love her fellow man. I kind of hoped that would sum up everything she would need to know."

He picked up another flat rock and skimmed it across the water.

"I used to be real good at skimming rocks. You see, Lord, I don't understand at all why any of this is happening. Why would you make her so perfect and then take her away from us? It just doesn't make much sense to me. And I'm asking you not to do that. I'm begging you not to do that."

Sam got on his knees by the shore of the lake and began The Lord's Prayer: "Our Father, which art in heaven..."

Back in Sam's front room, Dr. Riley laid out for Bonnie and Alex the bottom line of his diagnosis. He had consulted a specialist, a Dr. Sanjay Saxena, ."..one of the most highly regarded neurosurgeons in the world. Practices mainly at Cedars-Sinai in L.A., but he has a vacation home up here in White Dove. He has reviewed the information extensively and feels the tumor is very large and, uh, well,... he says it's inoperable. He seems to think that the tumor could be touching a place in the brain that could cause hallucinations. This could explain why she thinks she sees Jesus when no one else does."

Overhearing all this from their hiding place in the den were Danny and Sara. Neither of them really understood, but they knew this didn't sound good.

Bonnie asked, "What about the children she cured?"

"That could be explained," said the Doctor, "through a dramatic instance of induction in a form similar to the placebo-suggestion effect."

"You're suggesting some kind of mass hypnosis?" said Pastor Jenkins incredulously.

"A strong idea or image of healing in the minds of the children, coupled with an emotionally charged image of Jesus. It's possible."

The Pastor now found himself getting emotionally charged. "David, crippled children could suddenly walk again. A blind girl regained her eyesight. This little girl of ours cured cancer for crying out loud."

"Bob, I've done a lot of looking into this," replied Dr. Riley, "and what I don't think you realize – like most people don't realize – is that there are actual documented accounts that do explain these types of healings. Like one of the best-known cases in medical annals is the case of a Mr. Wright. Back in 1957, in Long Beach, California, this man had tumors the size of grapefruits throughout his body and had less than two weeks to live. He was given an inert substance that he believed was a cure for cancer. In four days he was well. All the tumors had disappeared. The case was published by Bruno Klopfer under the title, 'Psychological Variables in Human Cancer' in the Journal of Projective Techniques. So it's clearly in the realm of possibility that this is exactly what happened to those children."

Pastor Jenkins, now very uncomfortable, glared at Dr. Riley and was about to say something when Bonnie raised her voice: "Please, Doctor," she said, "What happened with the children can be discussed later. We're here for Sara now. So, you said it's 'inoperable.' What does that really mean?"

"I'm sorry, but we have to expect the worst."

"I don't understand," said Bonnie. "What other options do we have?"

"There are no options, Bonnie. I'm sorry," said Dr. Riley. "It's Dr. Saxena's opinion, and I concur with him, that the risks of surgery may be higher than the expectation of success."

"What exactly are you saying?" asked Bonnie. "Are you saying Sara's going to die?"

The Pastor interjected, "I don't think anyone can say for certain when she is going to die."

Now Bonnie was even angrier. "Dr. Riley," she said, "are you saying that my daughter is going to die? Just tell me, Doctor! Just tell me the truth!"

Dr. Riley bit his lip a little. It was a habit he had from childhood and delivering this kind of news was far and away the hardest part of his job. Finally, he nodded and said, "She's dying, Bonnie. Sara is dying. I'm so sorry."

Bonnie's entire body and soul resisted accepting this. "When I told you that Sara had said that Jesus told her he would be taking her to heaven, you said it was all in her imagination. That she was healthier than you or I and that she would outlive us both."

Dr. Riley nodded. "I know. But knowing what I know now, I think that subconsciously she knew she was dying and this, along with the tumor is probably what caused her to see this hallucination."

Bonnie was dumbstruck. Pastor Jenkins closed his eyes with furrowed brow.

"Bonnie," Dr. Riley continued, "Believe it or not, I know what you're going through and if I could change any of this, I would.... I just can't."

Sara, listening to this from the den, had teared up. She was trying to be brave and wiped her eyes, but the tears came anyway. Danny, put his arm around her and had to wipe away his own tears. Sara felt she may really cry out and she didn't want them to get caught, so she motioned to Danny and the two of them snuck quietly out of the den and back outside where they sat and huddled in the patio.

Bonnie was flowing with tears; Alex stepped over and hugged her. They were both beside themselves. Alex was more stoic. Someone had to be strong for his family.

"We need to get Sara," said Alex.

"We have to tell her."

"I know."

"I think it would be best," said Dr. Riley, "if Sara was hospitalized. If something happens, at least emergency medical care would be available. It's her best chance."

"You mean there's something you can do?" asked Alex.

"I'm saying we might be able to stabilize her condition in an emergency and allow her to live a little longer."

"But you're saying she is still going to die?"

Alex could see the answer in the doctor's pained face.

"How long does she have?" Alex asked. "At best?"

"I can't say. It could be weeks if we're lucky. Or, it could be a minute from now. There's just no way of knowing at this point."

Bonnie couldn't take listening to this anymore. "We need to be alone with our daughter," she said and went into the kitchen.

The Doctor handed Alex a card and said, "I wrote my cell phone number on the card. I'm sorry. I'll reserve a room for her at the hospital."

Alex looked grimly at the Doctor and the Pastor as he took the card. They made their exit out the front door, leaving Alex to follow Bonnie to the kitchen, where they stood together, embracing, as she broke down and wept in earnest. They didn't see Danny and Sara watching them anxiously through the kitchen window. Finally, after a few minutes, Bonnie stopped and wiped away her tears.

"We have to be strong for Sara," she said.

Alex held her in his arms. "Being strong for you and for her is what gives me life. What are we going to tell her?"

"I don't know. I don't know anything right now."

Suddenly a tearful Sara burst into the room and put her arms around her parents. "It's okay, Mommy," she said. "I just don't want you to cry. Please don't cry. I heard what the doctor said about me dying. I just don't want you to cry. Please. It's okay if I go to heaven, I'll be with Jesus." Bonnie picked Sara up in her arms and held her. Then she saw Sam walk in to the kitchen.

"Dad, Alex will tell you what's going on. I may need you to watch Danny. We might have to take Sara to the hospital."

"I don't want to go to the hospital," said Sara. "I want to stay here. I want to go to the lake and see Jesus."

Bonnie saw that Danny, too, was weeping.

"Danny, I need you to stay here with Daddy and Grandpa. Sara and I need to talk in the bedroom."

Sara said, "I want Daddy to come, too."

"It's okay," said Sam, "I already talked to Dr. Riley out front. Danny and I will be fine. Won't we, Danny?"

Danny had no idea what to do. He watched his mother, father and sister walk away into the back bedroom. Suddenly he ran over to his Grandpa and hugged him as Sam got down on one knee to hold him to his chest.

"Is Sara going to die?" Danny asked.

Sam held him tight. "We're all going to die, Danny. We just don't know when."

"But the doctor said she could die today, or tomorrow and the longest would be in two weeks. I don't want her to die, Grandpa."

Sam patted Danny's back gently as he held him and rocked him a little. "Neither do I, Danny. Neither do I."

And Sara looked upset as she sat on the bed next to her mother. Alex pulled up the old wing chair next to the bed and sat close to Sara. Bonnie took her daughter's hand. Sara looked up and smiled at her father. Alex bent over and pushed back Sara's bangs.

"You are so beautiful," he said, "and I love you..." He held out his hands as far apart as he could... "this much!"

Sara spread her hands as far as she could. "And I love you this much times infinity!"

Bonnie smiled and took Sara into her arms and hugged her. When she let go, Sara looked at her, then at Alex, and said, "I don't want to go to the hospital. I want to go to the lake and find Jesus. Please!"

"Honey, we need you to be in the Hospital in case you get sick," said Bonnie.

"I know that's what the Doctor said, but I want to go to the lake. I want to ask him if I can go to heaven later and stay here with you until I grow up."

Bonnie gently cupped her daughter's face in her hands. "Honey, the doctor said you didn't really see Jesus. It was only a hallucination. You just thought you saw him. The image was in your mind and when the tumor touched the part of your brain that contains that image, it made you think you were seeing him."

"No, Mother. It wasn't in my mind. I saw Jesus."

"Please Sara, I don't know what I would do if something happened to you."

Bonnie just stared into her little girl's eyes. In the few moments that passed, Bonnie saw her entire life – not just Sara's but her own as well – flashing before her. All the years with Sara and all of her own years growing up all came now down to this and the thought of losing her precious child was too much; no matter how strong she tried to be, a tear rolled down her cheek.

Sara only wanted her mother to be not in pain; she reached up and wiped away Bonnie's tear. "It's okay, Mommy. We can go to the hospital."

Bonnie took Sara into her arms and they held each other as never before.

Pastor Jenkins stared grimly out the window of Dr. Riley's car as they drove home. "David, I think what you said back there was wrong."

"They have a right to know."

"Exactly. But to know what?"

"Alright, Bob, the truth is I don't know what happened to those children. And I don't know what Sara saw or if she actually saw anything at all. Okay?"

"Well, what if the little girl is right and you're wrong?"

"What difference does it make?" said Dr. Riley. "She said Jesus told her he would be taking her to heaven soon. Where does that leave her? You know something? I don't want to believe in a Jesus who takes our children from us."

Pastor Jenkins continued to stare silently out the window.

"The one thing I do know?" Dr. Riley continued. "All the prayer in the world isn't going to save Bonnie's daughter. The sooner she accepts that, the easier it will be."

Bonnie found it hard to say just what she really believed as she and Alex sat that night by Sara's hospital bed. Had she accepted Dr. Riley's belief in the futility of prayer? Not by a long shot. But was she ready to expect a miracle? She didn't dare count on it. Her daughter was dying and she was terrified near out of her mind. It was hard to argue against medical expertise when you had virtually none of it yourself. A straw can look like a lifeline when it's the only thing you have to grab onto.

Sam and Danny entered Sara's hospital room and Danny immediately ran to Sara and gave her a hug.

"We're going to go get something to eat," he said. "But we wanted to come by and see you."

"Dad, if you're going to go eat," said Bonnie, "I'll give you some money."

"I've got money."

"Sara, do you want anything?" asked Bonnie.

"A hot fudge sundae."

"If that's what you want," said Sam, "that's what you'll get."

"Could you get it at the Dairy Queen?" asked Sara.

"I'll go anywhere in the world to get you what you want. You want reindeer, elves, a flat tire. Just name it."

Sam had steeled himself to show Sara only his love and not his fear. Even Danny stepped up and instinctively followed his example. But once in the truck, the faces grew long and dismal.

And Sam found himself flashing on long-buried memories as if they had happened that morning. He was suddenly back in Vietnam near his base at Loc Ninh, close by Cambodia. His twelve-man Special Forces Recon Team had discovered that an American-friendly village they were about to enter had been captured by a platoon of North Vietnamese. No one noticed Sam's group as they quietly approached, because the NVA soldiers were focused on their task at hand: they were systematically bringing out the men of the village into the square and, one by one, they were executing them – along with their sons. Sam and his team watched the soldiers bring out a little girl who was the daughter of the leader of the village. Because the leader had no son, they were going to execute his daughter. Sam looked over at his childhood friend, Chuck Carter. They both knew that little girl; they had played soccer with her, as well as with many of the dead boys bleeding in the dust next to their fathers.

Sam and Chuck looked at the other men in their unit; they all nodded their heads yes, and they opened fire on the North Vietnamese regulars.

When the firefight ended, all of the NVA soldiers were dead. The Green Berets rushed into village square and Sam found the leader's little girl lying near death next to her father. He yelled for the Medic and tried every first aid trick he could. He fought hard to save her, but still, after fifteen minutes of CPR and tourniquets and salving and bandaging, the little girl bled out and died. Sam could still feel the pain of how helpless he felt then, and what struck him hard now, as he drove down the highway to the Dairy Queen, was that he felt even more helpless now, because he knew he had hit a wall.

There simply was no earthly thing he could do, no tool he could pick up, nor weapon he could wield that would work in the slightest way to save his beautiful little granddaughter. A tear was rolling down his cheek as he heard Danny yell out, "You missed the street. The Dairy Queen is back there."

When Sam and Danny arrived at the Dairy Queen, they found themselves standing in line at the order window, right behind little Theresa De La Paz and her mother, Maria. Theresa was the first to notice, as she turned around, recognized Danny and her eyes lit up. She herself was hardly recognizable. Her hair had started to grow back and she was healthy, vital and energetic.

"Hi! You're the one that was combing his hair on the front porch!"

Danny, shrugged, pulled out his comb, held it up and ran it through his hair.

"Where's your sister?" asked Theresa.

Danny stopped; he put the comb away, looking very glum. He looked up his Grandpa and didn't say anything.

"Maria, this is my grandson, Danny. Sara, the little girl who, I guess, healed your daughter, is my granddaughter. And, well,... at the moment, she's in the hospital.

Maria was surprised and saddened. "What's wrong with her?

"She's sick."

"How sick?"

"She has a brain tumor."

"Oh, no, I'm so sorry," said Maria.

"But that can't be," said Theresa.

"But it is," said Sam.

"But he was with her."

"Who?"

"Jesus was standing next to Sara and the blind girl," said Theresa. "That's when I knew my cancer was gone."

Sam hesitated. He didn't know whether to be amazed or get his hearing checked: "Wait. You... You actually saw him?"

"Yes."

"Jesus? You saw Jesus?"

"Yes! Jesus. He was standing right there with his hand on Sara's shoulder."

"And you... you're okay, right?"

"Yes, she is," said Maria. "As far as we can tell, completely. Thanks to your granddaughter. Sam, if there is anything Theresa or I can do for her...? Anything! I'm so sorry, Sam. I'm so sorry."

But Sam was so stunned by this news and his imagination raced so far ahead of him, that even though it took him another three minutes to get to the order window, it took him yet another minute to remember why they had come.

Maria was stunned to the quick, her heart catching in her throat as Sam's news brought back to her the most terrifying moment of her own life. That moment when the doctor walked into the waiting room and told her that Theresa had cancer. The doctor had gone on about how it was Hodgkins lymphoma but Maria didn't hear much of that as she felt like she had just taken a sledge-hammer blow to the forehead. In that instant, she was just trying to survive for what remaining time she would have with her daughter. Strangely, it was an even more horrifying moment than when she saw the Marine Captain in full dress uniform come walking up her driveway – an image that she knew could mean only one thing. Losing her husband, Carlos, in Afghanistan was crushing, made her sadder than she had ever been before. He was the love of her life. But the thought of losing the daughter they had made together, put her into an utter panic. "What am I going to do? What am I going to do?" she had kept thinking. And now, on hearing about Sara's fate, she could only thank God for the mystery of the healings that came through her and she prayed silently that Sara not be left out of the healings.

CHAPTER 18

Bonnie looked at her watch. "I wonder what's keeping them?"

"They'll be here soon," said Alex. "There's always a line at that place."

"Dad's right. It'll be okay. They're probably just eating my hot fudge sundae and thinking how good it tastes. While I lay here wishing I was eating it."

"If they're not back soon, Daddy will go get you one," said Bonnie.

"No, I want you both to stay here with me. Daddy, let's sing something."

"Okay, how about 'The Flying Purple People-Eater'?" said Alex.

Sara laughed. "No, how about that other song? But really sing it and Mommy and I will sing the Amen part."

"You mean, sing it like I did at the picnic?"

Sara loved singing. That's one of the things she loved about going to church. No one got more into the songs than Sara. She knew all the traditional hymns and most of the American Gospel songs, like "Amen, Amen," which Alex now led them through -- a simple, beautiful song that told the story of the life of Jesus. It was one of Sara's favorites. They were just getting into the final "Amen" chorus when Sam and Danny walked in carrying her hot fudge sundae.

Sara ate her sundae with gusto. "Mmmm, this is so good! Danny, you want some of this?"

"No, thanks," said Danny, "I had my own." Of course the truth was, he hadn't really. But he didn't have much of an appetite.

As the evening stretched on, Danny began to doze off in a chair and Bonnie, sitting on the bed next to Sara, ran her fingers through her young one's fine blonde hair.

"Do you know how beautiful you are?" Bonnie asked.

"Yes."

"Well, you're even more beautiful than you think you are."

Sara just smiled and looked at her Grandpa, who smiled back and said, "You're Mama's right, you know."

Bonnie then noticed Danny falling asleep. "Dad, he can't sleep like that. Can you take him home?"

"Sure," said Sam.

"Will you come back tomorrow?" asked Sara.

"There's nothing in the world could keep me away."

"What about a company of Marines?"

"Not be the day they would want to run into me."

"How about a tank?"

"Wouldn't want to be the driver."

"I love you, Grandpa."

Sara and her Grandpa understood each other. The same love and, yes, the same sadness showed in both their faces.

So Bonnie and Alex stayed in the room with Sara while Sam took Danny home. Bonnie sat on the bed next to Sara and gently ran her fingers through Sara's fine golden hair.

When Sam got home to the ranch, he carried his sleeping grandson into the house and put him to bed. But sleeping was the last thing Sam was able to do. One A.M. found him sitting under the light at the kitchen table staring at the big old family Bible he had dusted off and spread out.

After a couple hours he looked up and saw Danny standing next to the table, quietly waiting to be noticed. He couldn't sleep either.

"Why don't you come sit down here and I'll make some hot chocolate."

"Do you have the good stuff?"

"Yeah, I've got the good stuff."

As Sam got up, poured milk into a pan and began to heat it up, Danny grew more agitated.

"I'm worried about Sara."

"So am I, Danny. But she'll be okay."

"But she's not going to be okay. She's going to die, Grandpa."

"We don't know that."

"I heard the doctor tell Mom that she was going to die."

Sam reached up to a shelf and took out some powdered chocolate and a seventy-percent chocolate bar. He put three teaspoons of powdered chocolate into the milk. He broke off a piece from the bar and placed it into the milk. He stirred the chocolate.

"Well,... let's drink some chocolate," said Sam, "and we'll talk about it."

So Sam Donovan and Danny Hopkins sat at the kitchen table, huddled over their respective mugs of the good chocolate and they sipped, late into the night.

Finally, Sam said, "I've been thinking about what the doctor said. And I think he's wrong."

"Why?"

"Well, if the tumor was causing your sister to see Jesus, how did little Theresa see him?"

"I don't know. Wait. I know. Because he was really there?"

"Exactly."

"But Grandpa, even Jesus told Sara he would be taking her to heaven."

Sam nodded. "I've thought about that as well. But I figured that, sure, he might not listen to me or you, but he might just listen to Sara."

"So we should take her to the lake."

"That's kind of what I was thinking," said Sam. He took another sip of chocolate. "Problem is, I don't think your Mom and Dad are going to let us take her out of the hospital. Not that I can blame them, really. After all, they're not so sure Sara even saw Jesus."

"What about Theresa?" said Danny. "Maybe if Mom and Dad knew Theresa saw Jesus, too,... then... maybe they'd believe Sara. And then they'd let us take her to the lake."

The Mustard Seed

"Well now," said Sam, nodding slowly. "That gives us something to sleep on, doesn't it?"

Then Danny gave Sam a quizzical look. "Grandpa, why couldn't I see Jesus when I was at the lake with Sara? Did I do something wrong?"

"Well, of course I couldn't see him either, and I guess that very question has occurred to me, too. I guess I don't rightly know. But...what I do think is pretty clear is that God works in ways that we sometimes flat-out don't understand. I think he has some purpose for Sara. And in the end, I guess it's all about faith, isn't it?"

Danny scratched his head and finally nodded. "Think we could watch TV on the couch?"

"Sure," said Sam and the two of them settled in to watch 'Raiders of the Lost Ark' until Danny dozed off about three A.M. Sam carried him to bed and then tried to get a few winks himself. Didn't succeed much, though. His mind wouldn't let him. A torrent of emotions carried him away. His fear of losing Sara pulled him one way only to be turned inside out by the hope that Jesus could do for her what he had done for the others. If in fact that's what had happened. And then there was the sea of doubts on which he tossed and turned in what remained of his short night, questioning every decision he had ever made in his life and wishing he had spent more time with Bonnie and with his grandchildren and pondering how he would do things differently, given the chance. Okay, he knew he wasn't Ebenezer Scrooge, never had been. But still, he regretted the loss of time with the ones he loved.

And it suddenly occurred to him: maybe he was just spiritually blind. He never thought of that before. Would that explain why he couldn't see Jesus?

For Sara, the next morning, nothing had changed, except for maybe the appearance of a blue shadow under her eyes that made her look weary and wan. Other than that, she began this day in her hospital room as she had ended the last one: "Daddy, let's go to the lake! Please?!"

Alex hesitated as he glanced at Bonnie. "Maybe we should."

"Yes, please!" said Sara.

"Alex, no," said Bonnie, "No, we can't do it." Bonnie turned to Sara. "Sweetheart, I can't take care of you at the lake. We have to stay here."

"Please, Mom."

Then Dr. Riley entered, carrying a large, pink, stuffed bunny and accompanied by a distinguished-looking Indian man in his fifties, whom he introduced as Dr. Sanjay Saxena.

After the brief handshakes and pleasantries, Dr. Saxena asked Sara if he could "borrow your mother and father for a moment. There's something I would like to show them. Doctor Riley could stay here with you and I promise I won't keep them long."

Sara reluctantly said, "Okay," not really wanting them to go.

"We won't be gone long," said Alex. "I promise."

"Okay, Daddy."

Suddenly Pastor Jenkins entered, along with Fathers Echevarria and Moretti. Sara greeted them all with a cheery but somewhat puzzled, "Hi."

"Hope you don't mind us coming by?" said the Pastor. "Father Echevarria and Father Moretti wanted to meet you."

"I don't mind," said Sara. "Are you priests?"

"Yes," said Father Echevarria, "I work in Mexico and Father Moretti here lives in Rome and is visiting me. The little girl with cancer you healed in your front yard? That was my niece. I wanted to thank you."

"You're welcome."

Bonnie said, "We'll be right back."

"Okay, Mom."

As Dr. Saxena took the Hopkins' out via the hallway, Dr. Riley, suddenly realizing that he was still standing there with a large pink bunny, stepped over and handed it to Sara.

"Thanks."

"I hope you like the color."

"I like pink."

"How are you feeling, Sara?" asked Pastor Jenkins.

"I feel okay. I want to go to the lake."

Dr. Riley looked at her and said, "Sara, there's nothing I'd want more than for you to be able to go to the lake. But for now,

I think it would be better if you stayed here."

"No, it wouldn't be better," said Sara. "Don't you believe in God?"

Dr. Riley was a little taken aback. "Yes, but God helps those who help themselves."

"No, Doctor," she said. "God helps those who have faith. If you just have the faith of a mustard seed you can move a mountain."

The two priests looked at each other and couldn't help but smile a little as Sara turned to Pastor Jenkins.

"Isn't that right, Pastor Jenkins?"

Dr. Riley gave his old friend a look that said, "Don't you dare."

But the Pastor just smiled. "You can say to the mountain, 'Move from here to there' and it will move. And nothing will be impossible for you. That is what we believe, isn't it?"

Dr. Riley was silent.

Father Echevarria smiled at Sara: "No one could have said it more beautifully, Sara."

The Doctor appeared a little a perturbed as he realized he was being outgunned. Not something he was used to on his own turf. Let alone by an eight-year-old. As he turned and stepped toward the door, Sara said, "Thank you, Dr. Riley."

As the Doctor turned back and looked at Sara, holding the pink bunny and smiling at him, he found it impossible to stay perturbed about anything and found himself smiling back at her.

"I hope you like the bunny," he said.

"I love it."

When Dr. Riley left the room, Sara stole a glance at Father Echevarria then looked back at her stuffed pink bunny. For all her sweetness, she was really a shy little girl.

"It wasn't me who healed your niece."

"I know that," Father Echevarria said, "but it was through you that our Savior chose to work. And I saw the joy in your face when the blind girl got her sight back."

"Did you see how happy her mother was?"

"Yes, I did."

Meanwhile, down the hall in an office, Dr. Saxena was showing Sara's X-rays to Bonnie and Alex. He pointed out the way the tumor interweaves itself through the folds of the brain.

"You can see where the growth is set at the brain stem," said Dr. Saxena. "This is what we think is causing the visual hallucinations. From there it runs through the cerebellum. At first I didn't think it was operable. I now think that even though some may believe it contra-indicated, there is a chance... a... a chance... that we might be able to remove it in surgery." The Hopkins' eyes grew suddenly large. "How dangerous would it be?" asked Bonnie.

"Well, it's high risk. There is a chance she may not survive the surgery. That is possible. But it's the only chance she has."

"I want to talk to Sara before we make this decision," said Alex. Bonnie agreed. "I would like to do another CT scan this afternoon," said Dr. Saxena, "to make sure there isn't any new growth, then perform the surgery in the morning. The longer we wait the greater the odds are against us. I know this is very difficult, but I don't see any other choice."

"Yeah, we understand," said a sullen Alex, "Thank you, Doctor."

As they got up to leave, Bonnie looked Dr. Saxena in the eye and asked, "You said it's high risk. What does that really mean? What are her chances? Fifty-fifty? What?"

Dr. Saxena looked at Bonnie for a moment. He was measuring the amount of frankness she could take. Not all parents really want to know. But Bonnie was coming on like a freight train. "It would be less than that. But as long as there is a chance, we should take it. As I said, it's the only chance she has. Without surgery, she will die."

"But she might die in surgery. And that would take away what little time I have to spend with her. Wouldn't it?"

Dr. Saxena nodded.

Bonnie turned to her husband. "We need to go talk about this."

"Look, I have to go make a call about another patient," said Dr. Saxena. "Why don't you stay here and talk? I'll be back in fifteen minutes or so. Okay?"

The Mustard Seed

The Hopkins' nodded and sat back down on the couch as the doctor left the room. Bonnie closed her eyes and put her face in her hands. Alex sat with furrowed brow and pondered.

"When I was a little girl," said Bonnie softly, now leaning back and staring out the window into the distance, "I remember playing in my mother's kitchen. I shadowed everything she did, sweeping the floor, baking cookies, trying to help her make her fabulous dinners, all those kinds of things. And I'd follow her around the house and when she went shopping at the market she'd take me with her and she would show me how to read labels, how to look for quality, how to get the best price. And people -- she taught me how read them; she was kind of psychic. Didn't call it that, but she knew she was and so did I. And she taught me how to treat people. Took me to Church just about every week. She taught me everything. And I remember being like six and thinking that I wanted to someday be just like her."

"You are just like her," said Alex.

"Yeah, well that's the thing, I never doubted that I would be. I wanted so badly to be a mother. That's why I was so happy when Danny was born. But all my life I felt I would be incomplete until I had a daughter. So I could give her...well, so I could give her what my Mama gave me. Then Sara came along and my life was perfect. So perfect... I never imagined anything like... I mean...I am not ready for this."

"Who can be ready for this?"

"Honey, what are we going to do?" Bonnie struggled to keep the tears from completely overtaking her.

"She's our baby," said Alex. "Our job is to make decisions for her that she is -- presumably -- not wise enough yet to make for herself. But who really has the wisdom here? I mean when you look at what she's already done...who are we to tell her that her instincts are wrong?"

"You mean -- ?"

"I mean what if we took her to the lake?" said Alex.

"They say that would be dangerous."

"So is not taking her to the lake."

CHAPTER 19

Sam Donovan pulled up his truck in front of Mark Miller's house. Danny bounded out of the truck, ran to the porch and rang the bell. Young Mark opened the door and stood there, looking like he'd never been sick a minute of his life.

"Danny!" Mark hadn't seen him since the day Sara touched him.

"Hi, Mark. Is Ellen home?" said a breathless Danny.

"Sure, what's up?"

"I'm trying to find that girl she used to hang out with. The one who had cancer?"

"You mean Theresa?"

"Yeah, well, Theresa saw Jesus the day that my sister healed her. And now Sara's in the hospital, dying. Grandpa thinks Theresa can help."

Mark's jaw dropped at the stunning news and he immediately wanted to ask all the usual questions that anyone would want to – "How?" and "Why?" and "When did this happen?" and all of that – but as he looked at the hyperventilating Danny and saw Grandpa, looking grim in the truck cab with the motor running, he knew this was not the time.

"I'll get my sister," said Mark. And he didn't walk, he ran toward Ellen's room.

When Alex and Bonnie returned to Sara's hospital room they found Sara all smiles playing tic-tack-toe with Father Moretti. Bonnie rushed over to her and kissed her on the cheek. "This is Father Moretti," said Sara. "He lives in Rome and wants me to visit him. He said his parents have a big house there and we could all stay with them as long as we like."

"That's on the other side of the world, Sweetheart," said Bonnie.

"He said he would show us Rome and give us a personal tour of the Vatican. Isn't that where the Pope lives?"

"Darling, we can talk about that tomorrow," said Bonnie. "But right now I need to talk to you."

Alex turned to the Pastor and the Two Priests. "We need a little time alone with Sara."

"Of course," said Father Echevarria. He and Father Moretti joined Pastor Jenkins and they all moved to the door.

"I need to visit some other patients here," the Pastor said to Bonnie. "I could stop by later if either of you need to talk."

Father Moretti winked at Sara. "I'll come by and see you tomorrow and don't forget next time you go to the lake you have to take me with you."

"Okay," said Sara.

With the room to themselves, Alex and Bonnie sat on the bed on either side of Sara.

Alex began. "The doctors think there is a chance if you have surgery they can remove the tumor."

"They want to operate," said Bonnie. "The doctor said there's a chance he can save you."

Sara looked at them with some bewilderment. "What does that mean?"

"It means," said Alex, "that there is a chance that–"

"It means," Bonnie interjects, "it has to work because I don't want to lose you. Ever."

"Can I die?"

Bonnie couldn't stop her eyes from welling. Sara reached up and wiped away Bonnie's tears.

"It's okay, Mommy. Don't cry." Sara was scared. "If this is what you want, I'll do it."

Bonnie took her in her arms and held her little girl against her cheek, wet with tears. Alex took them both into his arms and held them.

Not far away, Maria and Theresa sat in the front room of their home and watched the TV intently as Dolores Clark kept up her coverage of Sara's story:

"Little Sara Hopkins is going into surgery tomorrow morning. Her Doctors have not commented publicly on her condition, but according to my sources close to the family, this is a very dangerous surgery. Nevertheless, it's her only chance for survival, as without the surgery, it appears her death would be certain. I'm asking everyone to please pray for Sara Hopkins. God heard Sara's prayers for our sick children. Maybe he'll hear our prayers for her."

Back at the TV Newsroom, Jacob Colson dropped his breakfast burrito from his suddenly open mouth as he watched Dolores on the air monitor. "Yet again!...

That woman is trying to get me fired!"

Theresa and Maria watched Dolores, then looked at each other, squeezed each other's hands, and both blessed themselves with the sign of the cross and began to pray for their friend, Sara.

Sam and Danny saw the same broadcast on Mark Miller's IPad, as he and his sisters had crammed into the back seat of Sam's truck cab. The broadcast didn't make Sam happy.

"Let's pray, Grandpa," Danny said. "I don't want Sara to die."

"Yeah, we'll pray," said Sam. "And I don't mind her asking people to pray for Sara, but that little girl doesn't need to hear that her chances of survival are not good. For that matter, none of you need to hear it either."

"Oh, don't worry, Mom won't let her watch the news," said Danny, "And I'm starting to get a little faith in Jesus. So we're all going to pray, right?"

And pray in the truck they all did and in that moment, in the wake of the Clark broadcast, they were joined, though they had no way of knowing it yet, by all of the families of the children Sara had cured, plus uncountable legions of TV viewers in White Dove and in many thousands of other places across the region and the country and indeed around the world, as Sara's story went viral with every passing moment.

Five minutes later, Sam parked his truck in the driveway of the De La Paz home and waited. Ellen knocked on the door of the house and when Theresa opened the door, she found not only Ellen, but Sylvia, Mark and Danny on her porch. It didn't take the kids long to know what it was they would have to do.

Then came the inevitable call that Jacob Colson had dreaded. He could see on the caller I.D. that it was Bob Warman, V.P. of Network News. "Why me?" he thought. "I've kept my nose clean, done everything right for twenty years. Now this is how it ends." He gulped and picked up the phone and blurted out, "Listen, Bob, it won't happen again, trust me!"

"Well, I know that," said Warman, "but we have to make hay while the sun shines. I see now what you folks are doing out there and this miracle thing is pure genius! I love it!...Are you there, Jake?"

"Uh, yes! Yes!" said the stunned Jacob.

"And asking for the prayers, what a touch! That's incredible! Did you come up with that yourself?"

"Well, you know, I maintain a close, uh –"

"I mean, within minutes of the broadcast," Warman raved on, "this thing went viral; we're getting phone calls and emails from people praying for her from all over the country, plus Mexico and Europe -- even from Australia and Africa. Twitter and Facebook are going nuts! This little girl is pure gold and this Dolores what's-her-name is a star! Get me more coverage!"

"Yessir. Right away, sir!" Jacob was so relieved and grateful, he almost started praying himself.

CHAPTER 20

Bonnie sat on a bench by the hospital parking lot, hunched over, warming her hands on a cup of coffee. Pastor Jenkins sat next to her. She was clearly frightened. Near out of her wits, but not quite.

"Pastor, I don't know what I'm going to do."

"What does Sara want?" the Pastor asked.

"She wants to go to the lake and find Jesus. But if we go and something happened to her....You heard what Doctor Riley said."

"I can't advise you on this. It's something you have to decide for yourself." He took a deep breath. "But, in my humble and strictly personal opinion, Dr. Riley is a good doctor, and of course, I love him, but...well, he's not always right. And he may not be the best one to advise you either."

"How do you mean?" said Bonnie.

"Well, there was his son."

Bonnie looked at him uncomprehendingly.

"You do know Dr. Riley's son died of a brain aneurysm, right?"

"No, I didn't."

"He never gave up hope or stopped praying for his son. But when he died I think he lost his faith in God."

"But he's at church every Sunday," said Bonnie, "and the two of you are friends."

"I think he might just come to church for his wife's sake and he can't stop seeing me. We grew up together."

"Why didn't I hear about it?"

"It was just before you moved back here," said the Pastor.

"My Dad never said anything."

"Probably didn't know. He never came to town much after you left. I've never seen him in church."

Bonnie understood. "He has his own way about him."

"I really believe Dave Riley would give his life for Sara. But there's only so much that medicine can do."

She stared into the trees across the parking lot. "I don't know what to do."

"Trust your heart, Bonnie. Just trust your heart."

CHAPTER 21

The trail through the woods led to a world that seemed like no other. Maria and Theresa followed Sam and Danny, along with Mark, Sylvia and Ellen. Maria especially marveled at the beauty of the surroundings. Then they arrived at the lake, and they were awe-struck. Danny walked to the place by the shore where Sara had prayed for the bird. The others followed.

"Sara prayed right there," said Danny. "She kept saying the Lord's Prayer over and over again. Then she just sat there and didn't say anything. I caught four fish. Then she asked if I could see him. But I didn't see anything. Then the dead bird got up and flew away."

Sam looked around and scanned the lake. Everything was still as glass, but for a pair of mallards in the cove on the opposite shore. He had done this many times before, but only in search of birds and flowers and clouds and sunbeams in his rituals that others might call meditation. He just called it clearing his head. But this time he was searching for something else – a glimpse of something that he couldn't quite find. No, he saw only his familiar favorite view. Jesus made no appearance today. At least not to him.

But Theresa quietly stepped forward and stood by Danny. Then she got on her knees, made the sign of the cross and began to pray, "Our Father, which art in heaven, hallowed be thy name. Thy kingdom come, thy will be done on earth as it is in heaven."

The gray-haired nurse nodded to Alex and Bonnie when she came in to the hospital room and introduced herself to Sara. "Hello, I'm Susan. I need to take a little blood."

"Is it going to hurt?" Sara asked.

"A little, but just for a moment."

"Okay."

Nurse Susan wrapped a rubber band around Sara's arm. Sara closed her eyes and braced for the pain. But there was hardly any. Nurse Susan was very good with a needle and rightly proud of it. She had a way with veins. Locals who knew would schedule any needed blood tests to coincide with her shift.

"I'm sorry," she said, "but that's it. It won't hurt any more."

She filled up one vial full of blood, then another and another. Then she pulled the needle out of Sara's arm and taped some cotton to the wound.

"Done. Now put your finger here on the cotton and bend your elbow."

Sara did as she was told. She didn't want to cause anyone any problems.

Alex stood at the window and stared at the mountains in the distance. At certain moments, he found himself avoiding looking too much at Sara. He had to admit it, if only to himself, that he was desperately afraid for his beautiful little girl, shaking in his Nikes. And what he feared most immediately was that he would lose it in front of Sara and make her more scared than she already was. That was something he could not live with. He needed to be strong. So Alex became Clint Eastwood – as stoic as a rock. Finally he stole a casual peek at her.

"You didn't cry," said the Nurse. "I'm so proud of you. I'll stop by and see you later, okay?"

"Okay."

As the nurse left the room, Bonnie sat down on Sara's bed and held her hand. Bonnie couldn't help but notice that Sara seemed to be suddenly more tired than before and the circles under her eyes had become more pronounced; she was looking increasingly sick and fragile. Bonnie didn't want to focus on it, but there it was.

At the lake, Theresa was still on her knees and still kept repeating the Lord's Prayer: "Give us this day our daily bread..."

And as the day wore on, Alex played tic-tac-toe with Sara. He played O and she played X. When she won, she laughed and clapped her hands: "I win! I win!" Alex made sure that she won every time.

It was now Bonnie's turn to go to the window. She turned her face away from Sara, struggling to keep the torrent of her grief from overflowing into her child's face. The view of the mountains in the distance seemed so peaceful.

It was at the foot of those mountains that Theresa continued to pray. Sam stood next to Maria as she looked on while her daughter kneeled by the lake – the beautiful, shining water, broken only by a pair of mallards. But Theresa saw something more.

"He's here," said Theresa. "He's on the lake."

Maria knelt down next to Theresa, blessed herself with the sign of the cross and silently prayed. A few minutes passed. Finally Maria said, "I don't see anyone."

"I don't see him either," said Danny. He walked over to Theresa and knelt next to her, hoping that maybe that would help him see.

But it was Mark who said, "I see him, too!"

Now Sylvia knelt next to Theresa, as did Ellen, who asked Sylvia, "Do you see him?"

"Yes!" said Sylvia, seeming surprised that she could. "Yes, I can."

Danny now came and positioned himself next to Sylvia. Maybe this was the spot. But no. Danny saw nothing. "I must take after you, Grandpa, 'cause I don't see him."

"I don't either," said Maria, scanning the lake and the woods on the other side. "There's no one there."

"I wish I could say different," said Sam, "but I can't." All he saw was the mountains, the light on the water, the trees, the birds, even a whitetail buck stepping out of the thicket for a drink then lifting his rack and staring at Sam from across the lake. Just not Jesus.

Unlike the vision of Theresa, Ellen, Mark and Sylvia: they all saw Jesus. Clad in a white tunic and red mantle and bathed in a bright white halo of light, they saw Jesus walk past Maria and Sam as he approached the children. And each of them saw and felt him lean down and touch them on their heads in a blessing overflowing with love.

The frustrated Danny could see only the other children, looking up in awe and rapture. "Is he still there?"

The other kids saw Jesus turn and walk back out onto the lake until he disappeared in a seeming mist. And the children all breathed a collective sigh, not of relief but more the kind of sigh you make as you get off a giant rollercoaster, touching yourself to make sure you're still all there. But this was like no thrill ride any of them had ever imagined, leaving them at once breathlessly elated beyond imagining and at the same time drenched in a peace that embraces all experience.

Seeing that the four were left without words or breath, Danny asked, "So he's gone?"

Sylvia nodded.

Danny just looked at them and shook his head. "I don't know. It's not fair. I really wanted to see him."

Theresa was manifestly filled with purpose as she got on her feet and focused on Sam and her mother. "We have to go get Sara and bring her back here!"

"I believe them, Grandpa," said Danny. "But we need to hurry, don't you think?"

And old Sam found himself sharing his little grandson's logic. He looked out at the lake. He hadn't been able to see anything either. But when he looked back at the kids, it occurred to him that maybe not everybody was going to see Jesus the same way. Maybe that didn't mean he wasn't there. Maybe for some reason it fell to Sam to be like most people and to see Jesus not walking on water but in the faces and the actions of these kids – these knowing innocents who had somehow come to bring Jesus into their everyday world.

"I believe them too," said Sam. "We'll go back to the hospital and try to convince your mother and father."

Maria gave him a look of approval, but at the same time she hadn't the remotest clue as to how exactly they were going to do that.

"This ain't going to be easy," said Sam, by way of response to the unspoken question on Maria's face.

In Sara's hospital room, Bonnie and Alex held her hand and stroked her hair while they all ate from a plate of cookies that Dr. Riley's wife, Elizabeth, had made.

"I hope you don't mind," said Elizabeth. "I just wanted to come by and see you. I thought Sara might like some chocolate chip and pecan cookies. If she's going into surgery tomorrow, I know she can't have anything after ten o'clock. Figured now would be a good time to spoil her. It's the same recipe my Mama used to make for me when I was feeling blue."

"They're very good," said Sara. "Thank you."

In the hospital hallway, Sam said as they approached Sara's room, "Now, Danny, this needs to be handled... a certain way. So, just let me do the talking when we go in there."

"Okay, Grandpa."

Sam and Danny stepped into Sara's room. Pastor Jenkins and Fathers Echevarria and Moretti were there visiting with the Hopkins'. But Danny, cheerfully forgetful of his promise to stand back, immediately bounced over to Sara and blurted everything out. "People! Theresa, Sylvia and Mark and Ellen all saw Jesus! He was at the lake!"

"What do you mean they saw Jesus?" said Bonnie.

"They saw him at the lake!" said Danny.

"Okay, calm down, Danny. Dad, what's going on?" said Bonnie.

"I can't say for sure, but we ran into the little girl who had cancer that was healed in front of your house. She said she saw Jesus standing next to Sara at the house. So we took her to the lake and she said she saw Jesus there, too. And I believe her."

"Mark and Sylvia and Ellen saw him, too!"

Sara sat up.

Bonnie asked Danny, "Did you see him?"

"No."

Sara grabbed her mother's hand. "Please, Mom. Please, Dad. I know he's there."

"Ask Theresa!" said Danny. "And Mark and Sylvia and Ellen!

"Okay, where are they?" asked Alex.

"Just a minute," said Danny. He ran out of the room into the hallway and returned a moment later, leading Theresa by the hand, followed by Mark, Sylvia and Ellen. "Tell them," said Danny.

"He's telling the truth," said Theresa. "Jesus is at the lake."

Before Bonnie and Alex could catch their breath, Danny jumped up and stood on Sara's bed and yelled, "Everyone! Listen! We have to take Sara to the lake. I believe Jesus is there waiting for her and I have faith he's going to make her well."

"So do I," said Sam.

Alex looked at Danny and then at Sam and he stepped up: "So do I."

"So do I," said Elizabeth Riley.

"And so do I," said Pastor Jenkins

Everyone started to talk at once in a cacophony of reason outdistanced by emotion and sheer volume. Finally Bonnie stood up and shouted. "Hold it! Hold it! Everybody stop!" And amazingly they did.

"Has everyone forgotten what Jesus told Sara? He would be taking Sara to heaven soon. That's what she said he told her! Now I'm not going to give her up without a fight. I don't want to lose her."

Bonnie was virtually trembling with fear. "Now," she said, "can we all talk outside? In fact will all the adults please join me in the hallway?" The adults began to file out of the room with Bonnie. All but Sam.

"You, too, Dad," said Bonnie.

Sam shrugged and winked at Sara as he went out and joined the adults, looking like a little boy about to be scolded.

Sara and Danny shared a look of concern. "What if they don't let me go?"

Danny watched the door close on the adults and as he thought about it, his face turned to a frown. "You know... I don't think they will. They're thinking like adults."

Yes, this called for something special. Something they hadn't tried before. Danny looked so intensely at Ellen it made her uncomfortable.

"What?" said Ellen.

"You're tall," said Danny.

"So?"

"Can you drive?"

"You mean like a car?"

"Yes, like a car."

"Maybe," said Ellen, "I guess. I mean, I've never tried. Anyway, what's the point? We don't have a car."

"Get ready, Sara," said Danny. "We're leaving." He reached into Bonnie's purse, which had been left on the nightstand, grabbed her keys and tossed them to the surprised Ellen.

"Wow," said Ellen as she held the keys gingerly. "Do you know how much trouble we're going to get into?"

"I'll take the blame," said Danny. "Let's go."

Panicked, Ellen looked at the other kids.

"It's for Sara," said Mark.

Ellen got it. She sighed, nodded and said, "Okay. Let's go do some driving."

As Sara got out of bed, she almost slipped and fell but Mark and Sylvia were there to catch her. Danny poked his head into the hallway. He saw the adults gathered down the hall to the left, so he quietly gestured that they should all exit to the right. Danny and Sara and Theresa and the Miller kids all walked quickly around the corner to the nearest exit. Fortunately, they were on the first floor of this small hospital. As soon as they got outside, they moved as fast as they could with an increasingly weakened Sara in tow. Finally, they got her to Bonnie's blue Ford Explorer and they all climbed in, pulling Sara with them.

Ellen fumbled bravely with the keys and settled nervously into her task of orienting herself to the cockpit and trying to learn to drive, while the realization sank in that she would actually be responsible for the lives of five passengers.

"I can't believe I'm doing this," Ellen muttered to herself. "My first time driving a car and I'm probably breaking about eighteen different laws before we even get out of the parking lot."

"Don't worry," said Danny, "I'll keep a lookout for the cops."

"Right. Perfect. Glad we got that covered. What could go wrong?" said Ellen, all the while thinking this was the craziest thing she had ever imagined and that she had no idea what the penalties would be if she got pulled over, but that was probably a good thing because if she did know, she probably wouldn't do it and she had to do it because it was the perfect thing to do. It was for Sara. So, another deep breath later, Ellen turned over the engine, put it into gear and headed for the driveway. She cut the turn a little sharply and one rear wheel went up over the curb as the SUV lumbered side to side, but before they knew it, there were six kids on the state highway, heading for the lake to meet up with Jesus.

Meanwhile, Bonnie was aghast as she and the adults returned to Sara's now empty room where, through the window, her eye was caught by the sight of her own SUV bouncing off the curb and then speeding away down the road.

"Oh, my God! They've got my car and Sara's with them."

"They're going to the lake," said Maria.

Bonnie turned to her father. "This is your fault, Dad. You put these damned ideas in her head. If anything happens to her – " "Honey, I don't think I'm the one whose been taking her to church every Sunday and putting these... ideas into her head. But we can either stay here and talk about it or go after them." Bonnie was beside herself. "Let's go," and she stormed out of the room. Alex, Sam and Maria followed, along with Pastor Jenkins and the two priests. In the hall, the Pastor was buttonholed by Drs. Riley and Saxena.

"Where is everyone going?" asked Dr. Riley.

"The kids took Sara in Bonnie's car. They're on their way to the lake."

"We're coming with you."

"This is crazy," said Dr. Saxena. "Even if we go, if something happens, there won't be anything we can do."

"Are you coming?"

"Hell yes!" So, after the mad rush to the cars in the parking lot, it was Sam who led the way in his truck with Maria and Butch, who had waited patiently in the truck, followed by Alex and Bonnie in Alex's red pickup, then the Pastor and the priests in Father Echevarria's car and finally the two doctors, along with Elizabeth Riley, completed the caravan in Dr. Riley's Mercedes.

Ellen fought to keep control of the wheel of the SUV as she rolled down a dirt road. She hit a bump that threw the car off the road and they narrowly missed a tree as Ellen just did steer it back on to the road. Everyone in back was tossed all over.

Sara, in the back seat, asked, "Do you have a driver's license?"

"How would I have that? I'm twelve years old."

The next bump nearly knocked them into another tree. Everyone tried to hang on for dear life. Theresa reflexively blessed herself with the sign of the cross. Mark, with a worried look, noticed that Sara was looking very weak indeed and wasn't handling the rough ride all that well.

When Father Echevarria saw Alex's truck turn off the highway onto the dirt road, he made the turn himself a little too quickly and spun out, stalling his car in the process.

"Don't worry," said Pastor Jenkins, "You won't lose them. Just follow this road around that bend. There's nowhere else they can go."

Father Echevarria restarted, put the car in gear and as he headed for the bend, he saw Dr. Riley's car in the rear-view mirror. Meanwhile, Sam finally got to the end of the dirt road and pulled up behind Bonnie's Explorer. The kids had already gone on ahead.

"There," Sam pointed, "we have to take the old bike path to the lake."

"We'll follow you, Dad."

Bonnie and Alex followed Sam and Maria into the woods. A moment later Father Echevarria pulled up behind Alex's truck and parked just in time to see Sam, Maria, Alex and Bonnie disappearing along the bike path into the woods, with Butch right behind them. Doctor Riley pulled up and parked next to Father Echevarria's car. The two doctors jumped out along with Elizabeth and walked up to the priests and the Pastor.

"I haven't been to the lake in years," said Dr. Riley. "I'm surprised the old bike path is still here. We still have a ways to walk."

"When we were kids," said Pastor Jenkins, "David and I used to ride our bikes out here on the weekends."

The Mustard Seed

The kids had to move slowly through the woods. They had to wait while Sara stopped three times to catch her breath. Twice she almost fell down. Danny found himself wondering if he had done the right thing to insist on this lake trip. What if she couldn't get there? What if she just died right here? He could tell from Mark and Ellen's worried faces that they were thinking the same thing. That was not an idea Danny could accept.

Danny said to Mark, "Come on! We've got to get her there!" He and Mark each grabbed one of Sara's arms and pulled them over their shoulders so they could virtually carry her between them, all the way down the bike path through the trees.

Finally, with Sara leaning on Danny and Mark, the kids emerged from the woods and they found themselves at the lakeshore where Sara had prayed. Sara, with Danny and Mark's help, was able to make her way haltingly to the very spot where the bird had come to life. Then suddenly she got dizzy and asked them to put her down.

"Are you okay, Sara?" said Danny. "My head hurts and I'm dizzy. Let me kneel, okay?"

"Are you sure you're strong enough to kneel?" asked Danny.

"Yes!"

She knelt down. Sara was feeling more tired than she had ever felt before. But she knew Jesus was waiting for her, so she endured.

Then Danny knelt on one side of her and Mark and Sylvia on the other. Ellen and Theresa knelt next to Danny. Then together, they began to say aloud The Lord's Prayer: "Our Father, which art in heaven, hallowed be thy name. Thy kingdom come, thy will be done, on earth as it is in heaven..."

Elizabeth and the doctors, Pastor Jenkins and the Priests made their way through the woods along the nearly overgrown old bike path.

"Is this the right way?" asked a clearly uncomfortable Dr. Saxena.

"I think so," said Dr. Riley, "although I confess I haven't been here in a long time."

"It's the right way," said the Pastor.

"Shhh, listen," said Dr. Saxena.

They all stopped and listened. And they all heard faintly, carried on the soft wind in the trees, the sound of a chorus from far away: "Our Father, which art in heaven, hallowed be thy name..."

The group walked quickly down the winding wood path toward the haunting prayer in the wind. When finally they came out of the trees, they found themselves at the edge of the stunning lake and saw further up the shoreline, six kids on their knees and a sitting Black Labrador looking out at the lake. The children paid no notice to Alex and Bonnie and Sam and Maria, who stood back and watched them, nor to much of anything else beyond the object of their trance, even as the adults began to approach and stand next to them.

What immediately struck Father Echevarria was the look on the young ones' faces – pure awe and ecstasy. He shared a look with Father Moretti, who nodded in understanding. It is a look they had both seen before in other places, but most lately in Sara Hopkins' front yard.

"Are you seeing this?" Father Echevarria whispered to the Pastor.

And Pastor Jenkins nodded. "If there is any such thing as a beatific vision, these children..."

And indeed, if the children's eyes could have been shared, the vision they would have brought immediately to their elders would have been one of a bearded young man bathed in a white light, wearing a simple tunic and red mantle, walking toward them across the water. But of course, sharing the vision was not that simple.

"What are they looking at?" asked Dr. Saxena.

Bonnie wasn't sure of the answer, but she lowered herself onto her knees. Alex did the same. Sam noticed that even Butch had lowered himself to an alert "down" position as his eyes seemed to follow something moving. Sam now went to his knees.

"I don't see anything," said Dr. Riley.

Pastor Jenkins now went to his knees.

"Do you see something?" asked Dr. Riley.

"No, but the children look like they do," said Pastor Jenkins.

The two Priests had been watching the children and they agreed. The Priests, too, went to their knees.

"You're right," said Dr. Riley. "The kids look like they see something. I wish I could see something on this lake besides the water."

Elizabeth looked at her husband and slowly got down on her knees. Then Bonnie and Alex looked up from their prayer and they found themselves looking at Jesus, approaching them from across the lake.

The Pastor noticed that the children were no longer praying but simply staring out at the water. He turned to the lake and, found to his amazement, that he could see Jesus.

And so, to their own astonishment, could the Priests. During the work the Fathers had done for the Vatican Commission on Miracles, scenes of believers in a state of visionary ecstasy were a daily staple of their investigations. They had witnessed many such occurrences all over the world. But it was always from the outside, analyzing and judging the quality of what they could grasp of the believers' experiences, evaluating their claims. And sometimes this had bothered Father Echevarria. He had once confided to Father Moretti that he had felt like a kind of spiritual insurance adjuster. But now they were seeing it from the inside. And this was no longer about them imagining a vision. Now it was a vision that absorbed them into a dimension of being that rendered all their previous imaginings to be as matchsticks to the sun. There were no more questions now, only "the peace that passes all understanding" -- a phrase from St. Paul that the Priests and the Pastor had oft repeated in their sermons, but which only now they truly owned.

Dr. Saxena, of course, did not get to that place. He could see only a beach full of people and a dog staring into space with their mouths open. "I don't see anything," he muttered.

Pastor Jenkins, without removing his gaze from Jesus coming closer, said calmly and quietly to Dr. Saxena, "Open your mind, your heart and your soul and ask for his forgiveness, and maybe, just maybe you will see what we are witnessing."

Well, there was nothing in Dr. Sanjay Saxena's training

that seemed to offer any help. True, his family had brought from Mumbai a heritage rich in paranormal phenomena, but he was second generation in America and, somewhere between Harvard and the Royal Postgraduate Medical School at Hammersmith in London and his neurology practice in Beverly Hills, he had moved far from any of those beliefs. Yet here he was, faced with an empirical conundrum. All these people were experiencing something. Good grief, even the dog looked like he saw something: could he be the victim of a placebo effect, too? There were multiple healings now on record. Would it be logical to dismiss it all? The faces on these kids – and now on the adults – said no. So he lowered himself to his knees and closed his eyes, as he had seen the others do. And he prayed in silence. When he opened them, he still saw nothing, only the others with expressions of ecstasy in their visage.

What they saw was Jesus stepping onto the shore and moving toward Sara. Bonnie and Alex watched in awe as Jesus approached their daughter.

Sam was spellbound as tears welled in his eyes. "My God!" he thought, "I can see him!."

Pastor Jenkins and the Priests looked on serenely.

Elizabeth and Maria couldn't stop smiling.

Sara looked happily up at Jesus, who held her gaze and smiled at her. Moments passed. Then he picked Sara up in his arms and she, too, was now bathed in the same white light. Jesus turned and tenderly carried her back toward the lake as everyone stared in awe. He carried her out, over the water, whence he first appeared.

Dr. Saxena saw everyone staring out onto the lake and touched Dr. Riley's shoulder. "What are you seeing?"

"You can't see him walking across the lake with Sara?"

"No. She's still right there on her knees," said Dr. Saxena, pointing to Sara back on the bank.

But Dr. Riley never looked back. He just smiled peacefully as he, too, gazed at Jesus walking across the water with the beatified Sara in his arms. As Bonnie and Alex looked on, Sam wiped away a tear. Jesus kept walking toward the far shore with Sara's head on his shoulder. She looked back at her mother and father and seemed to wave.

Sam waved back. But was she waving... good-bye?

Everyone was full of tears as Jesus and Sara seemed to reach the far shore and they faded away into the trees.

Dr. Saxena still saw only Sara kneeling by the shore. Then, while the others were locked onto the far shore, he saw Sara go suddenly limp and fall to the ground. He jumped up and rushed over to her, only to find Sara's pulse so weak he couldn't really feel it.

"David!" he called out and Dr. Riley pulled out of his trance as he turned to respond and was shocked to see Sara lying on the ground. "Emergency room! Now!" said Dr. Saxena.

By now everyone had been shocked awake as if from the flight of a beautiful dream and were slammed suddenly with a very hard landing. Alex got to Sara first and picked her up in his arms. He felt like he was moving in slow motion and everything around him was a silent blur. It was like he had been lightning-struck and focused instantly and in toto on grasping the only thread of hope, however slim and tiny, that splayed out before him in that moment. He knew only that he must use every second to get Sara to the hospital. That was the only hope he had left and it was all the more precious.

Bonnie felt like she could barely breathe and was utterly dumbfounded. Through the windstorm in her head she heard Alex say, "Bonnie, let's take your car! There won't be enough room in my truck for Sara and the doctors."

Ellen held out the keys; Bonnie grabbed them and then she turned to Sam. "Can you get the kids home safely?"

"Yes," said Sam. "Just get Sara to the hospital. Hurry!"

Bonnie looked at Sam as tears began to roll down her face and she said, "She's gone, Dad. Sara's gone." As she heard those words come out of her mouth, Bonnie could barely believe she had said them. It felt like someone else talking. But she couldn't escape what she knew was the truth. The tears kept coming. As she turned and left the lake, every step she took back up the bike path toward the cars felt like a ton and her head was ready to explode. A moment ago Sara was in Jesus's arms and now --? While a part of her clung desperately to the hope that Sara would wake up, there was no escaping the image of Sara being taken away into the mist. Yes, it was Jesus taking her – taking her soul to heaven – as he had told her he would. And if her soul is gone, then what else could that mean but that she would not wake again? Not in this world. And her faith notwithstanding, Bonnie was crushed. "Oh, dear God, I've lost my daughter!" And she wept.

For the rest of the group, too, the ecstatic joy of the previous five minutes had turned into a train wreck, complete with shock, disbelief and disorientation.

CHAPTER 22

"I'm sorry, Bonnie," said Dr. Riley.

"I want to see her."

Alex stood up. "We want to see her now."

The others sat on chairs or milled about with sad patience in the crowded little emergency room waiting area. The Pastor and the Priests, Elizabeth, Sam and Maria and the children still couldn't believe what hit them. It was all so real. It seemed so perfect. How could this have happened?

Dr. Riley led Bonnie and Alex into the emergency room. Sarah lay in the bed on her back, a look of peace – almost a smile – on her face. Bonnie's breath caught in her throat and the tears began to roll as she looked at her little daughter, who poignantly, appeared now to Bonnie more beautiful than ever. She lay her head on Sara's chest and quietly sobbed. Alex bent over and put his arms around the both of them. Sam observed them from the doorway, finally turning away, trying unsuccessfully to stop his tears.

Bonnie finally gained a little control. She rose and took Sara up in her arms, the young mother with her face against the lifeless beauty that was her daughter. "Sara, my heart, my darling, I'm going to miss you so much." Alex hugged them both, his tears now pouring. Bonnie now wiped some of Alex's tears.

"Oh, God help us," said Bonnie. "Alex, what are we going to do?" And now she broke down in earnest and wept like a hurricane, her waters pouring over her dead child.

Dr. Riley had to leave the room to keep from breaking down himself. In the doorway he stopped and looked back at the family. He couldn't hold back the single tear that ran down his cheek; he knew what it was to lose a child. But he couldn't go there now. He owed it to the Hopkins to stay professional. When he turned to the hallway to exit, he saw Sam and Danny walking toward him.

"I'm sorry, Sam, I can't let anyone in the room other than her parents."

"David, you know me," said Sam. "Do you really think I'm going to let you keep this boy out of that room?"

Sam looked down at Danny and said, "You go on in there. No one is going to stop you."

Doctor Riley moved aside while Danny walked into the room. "Are you going in?" said Dr. Riley, "or should we give them some time alone with their daughter?"

"Won't go in, but I want to scc them together one last time."

Sam opened the door quietly and watched his family as Alex lifted Danny up onto the bed next to Sara.

"Daddy, is Sara going to wake up?"

"No, son, she isn't."

Danny began to cry. Alex held him and through his tears said, "Sara is gone to be with Jesus."

"That's where she always wanted to go, isn't it?" said Danny.

Alex nodded as he held his boy tightly, his remaining child. "Yes. Yes, it is, Danny."

Bonnie continued to weep heavily as she held Sara to her bosom and she called out to God in her agony. "Lord, I know she's with you. Thank you so much for showing that to us. I know we'll see her again. But it hurts so bad. Oh God, please help me. Please just give me the strength to get through this."

Now it appeared someone had heard her plea, because Bonnie heard a voice. "Mommy, don't cry. I don't want you to be sad."

Bonnie held out her daughter and looked at her. And sure enough, it was Sara doing the talking: "Don't cry. I asked Jesus if I could come back. So please don't cry."

"Oh, dear God, Sara!"

When Dr. Riley looked into the room and saw Sara talking, he started to rush in but Sam stopped him with an arm blocking the doorway.

"Like you said, Doctor, we should give them a little time alone with their daughter."

Sam shut the door as Sara wiped the tears from her mother's face.

"Mommy. Don't cry. I don't want you to be sad. Jesus said I could come home. He said you needed me. Don't cry."

"They're tears of joy, Sara, tears of joy. I'm so happy right now, I have to cry."

Happy tears ran aplenty around Sara's bed in that small room as Alex held his family in his wide embrace. The hope that Alex had clung to had come shockingly and gloriously true. And little Sara's happiness at being back radiated from her face like the very sun.

In the waiting room, as the word went around, her other loved ones slowly, quietly, as if guarding their relief against further disappointment, began to rise and filtered in to Sara's room and gathered around in growing awe and gratitude and pure joy that utterly washed away the loss they had felt only a few minutes ago.

Elizabeth Riley stood and watched with immense satisfaction as the Hopkins' and their supporters crowded around the little girl. She was profoundly happy for the Hopkins'.

CHAPTER 23

It was a new day in White Dove and the Hopkins Family gathered again at the hospital room where Sara had stayed overnight for observation, with Bonnie sleeping on a cot next to her. She wasn't about to let her daughter out of her sight. Not yet. Not just yet. Sam stood leaning against the wall, a silent arch-guardian over his family.

Then the Doctors came. Bonnie could see a glow of elation in their faces, even before they opened their mouths.

"We've run some more tests, including an MRI scan," said Dr. Riley, "and there is no sign anywhere of a tumor. It's gone."

"Completely gone!" said Dr. Saxena, almost dizzy with excitement.

"Yes," said Dr. Riley, "Sara is a perfectly healthy little eight-year-old girl." Sara's smile went from wide to wider.

"Do you think it would be okay," said Dr. Saxena, somewhat shyly, "if I went down to the lake with you sometime?"

"Okay, but your name isn't Thomas is it?"

"Oh, so you think I'm a doubting Thomas, do you?"

Sara just grinned, enjoying her little joke. And he, of course, laughed with her.

"Someone from administration will be up soon. She needs to get your parents' signature on a few forms and then you can go home."

"So, are you charging my mom and dad for this miracle?" asked Sara.

Dr. Saxena found himself compelled to smile broadly and even laugh out loud at this little sprite's pushy but adorable question. But then he thought about it a moment.

"No," he said. "No, you know something? I'll pick up any costs. I'll chalk it up to education. I've learned more from you in two days than I did in thirty years of medical training and experience. But can I still come to the lake with you?"

Sara nodded okay and it put a smile on Dr. Saxena's face as he left the room to face the world, feeling amazingly invigorated. Even Dr. Riley walked over to his wife, took her hand and watched as her face lit up.

"Heaven is so beautiful," said Sara. "I wish I could show it to everyone."

"Oh, I think you already have, Darlin'," said Sam. "I think you already have."

Dr. Riley turned to them. "You sure did for me, Sara."

"Oh, Dr. Riley?" said Sara.

"Yes, Sara?"

"When I was with Jesus," Sara said, "he brought me to meet a handsome young man wearing a blue track suit and he spoke to me. He said his name was Jesse and he told me to tell you that he loves you very much."

David Riley seemed to grow ten years younger on the spot. He took Elizabeth into his arms and they kissed, adding to the warm glow that encircled everyone in the room, as well as the group that had gathered in the hallway and lobby of the little hospital. And for Elizabeth, she had received the greatest news possible, for now she truly knew that her own child was not lost but only away for a while, and that in time she would be able to see him and hold him again, some place beyond the mist that had parted so briefly yet so stunningly on the lake that previous day.

And Bonnie was out-of-control giddy. She ran up to her father, threw arms around him and broke into tears of joy as she hugged him. "Thank you! Thank you so much, Dad, for believing in her! I don't know what would have happened if she didn't get to the lake. You did that. You saved her life."

"Yeah, you're partly right. I did that," said Sam. "But you're wrong about the other thing."

"What? How?"

"It was Sara – Sara with her faith -- who saved her life – and she saved my life. And from the look of things around here, a whole lot of other people's as well."

"'A lot of other people's lives as well,'" Father Moretti nodded and repeated to Sam. "You're right, but it wasn't just Sara. It was your faith, too. You should accept that."

Sam found the whole thing bemusing, and he was a little embarrassed by all the attention, but he had to admit to himself that it made him strangely proud – and very, very happy.

Neither he nor the Hopkins' had yet noticed that outside in the hospital's parking lot, crowds were beginning to gather around four microwave trucks that had raised their towers and set up broadcast facilities.

Two of the trucks were from local TV stations, one of which was Channel 14 – Dolores Clark's station – and the other two were CNN and Fox News. And more media were arriving by the minute. As Dolores sat in her truck, checking all her notes and prepped to go live, she knew that before the dust settled, there would be more news trucks, more coverage from all around the world. It had already been a huge day for her career. And when the latest call from Colson came in, she had to admit to herself that it felt good to have her boss eat crow and tell her to go large on the Hopkins story. Yeah, she knew in her heart that she knew a thing or two about what people want to see. She had broken the story and still felt she had an inside track because of her local connections. And yes, initially she had pangs of conscience about the family's privacy, but then Dolores thought, "The facts of the case are so spectacular, if God didn't want the publicity, why did he go and appear to so many people? No, really?"

Sara, fully dressed now, sat on the bed and said, "Grandpa? Mom said we could come over tomorrow."

"That's wonderful."

"I think we'll be coming over a lot, Grandpa."

"It's funny you should say that, because that's exactly what I've been praying for."

"I'll come over all the time, then."

Dr. Riley stepped back into Sara's room and approached Sam, gingerly, as he had learned to do over the years; even though this had to be one of Sam's better days, the Doctor figured one did not tap him on the shoulder or walk up behind him, lest a rib or jaw may accidentally be broken. Reflexes are hard to un-train. "Excuse me, Sam?"

"Yes?" said Sam with an angelic smile, to Dr. Riley's subtle relief.

"There's a crowd of media out front. You may want to get out through the back."

Sam nodded gratefully to the Doctor.

Bonnie came up and said, "Dad, my Explorer is looking very small and all these kids and everyone need a ride."

"I could take some of them," said Sam, "Wouldn't mind at all."

"How about you take Maria and Theresa home?"

"My pleasure," said Sam, and from the way he started smiling, it was clear to Maria that he really meant it. "I think I remember where you two live."

"I was hoping you would," said Maria.

"I said a prayer earlier," said Theresa. "I was asking that you would be the one giving us a ride."

"Well, it sounds like God's will then."

"That's good enough for me," said Maria.

"Me, too," said Sam.

But the next task now was to get Sara out of the building. Sam did a quick recon of the back route and found two things he didn't expect. In the back parking lot was Dolores Clark with her camera crew. Okay, that wasn't a big surprise, but what she was doing was. Standing in front of the video camera, Dolores was interviewing Chuck Carter, Sam's old Vietnam buddy who sat casually in a leather jacket on his old Fat-Bob Harley and spoke in quiet, measured tones, as if he wanted to make sure he was taken seriously. Now, Sam recalled at that moment that Chuck happened to be Dolores's second cousin – not so unusual in a small town like this. But why the interview? Sam stood quietly by and was entranced by what he heard.

Chuck told the rapt Dolores, "I had been exposed to Agent Orange during the war in Southeast Asia. Had various cancers ever since. Somehow I managed to survive. Then the latest diagnosis showed I had a pancreatic tumor. They said it was going to kill me pretty quick. The morning after I saw your report on Sarah Hopkins, I figured I had nothing to lose, so I showed up at her house, along with the crowd of others. I didn't have the nerve to go to the front; I let the kids do that. I just stood in the back and I prayed. I prayed like I never prayed before. I prayed for the faith to accept for myself the healing that I was witnessing among these kids. And I prayed to God for the strength to accept whatever happened, either way. Now, at the time, I thought I felt a little better, but I had no idea. Anyway, this morning, at my checkup at the VA Hospital, they couldn't find anything. No tumor, no nothing. Just healthy tissue."

Chuck wiped tears from his eye and shrugged. "Yeah. I am the happiest, the most grateful man in the world."

Sam's view of the scene grew blurry as his eyes welled with tears. When the interview was over and Chuck stepped away, Sam came toward him and called out, "Chuck!" The two men shared a look of recognition and joy and they ran to each other and embraced, like warriors who are amazed to find they have survived the final battle and they not only are alive but they have won and know they need no longer go to war and at last can put their swords to earth. As Sam held his old friend in a bear hug, he looked over to the side of the parking lot and saw Chuck's boys, Nick and Ryan standing nearby, tears running freely. Their whole aspect was very different from the cowering bullies Sam last saw back in Maria's Cantina. The boys seemed to Sam almost to glow, as though they, too, had been transformed by what they had witnessed.

"Good to see you again, Chuck," Sam managed to say, trying not to blubber too much. "You and your kids. You have a beautiful family."

"God bless you for yours," said Chuck, drying his eyes. "God bless you for yours."

Sam agreed. "Yeah. God has blessed us both." He nodded good-bye to Nick and Ryan as he went back toward the hospital's back door to go get Sara. And Sam thought, "Yes, Lord, you have blessed me big-time."

It was beginning to sink in to Sam that what had happened here was about more than two or three people getting healed and it was about more than a vision on a lake. This would be something big and far-reaching. Something very exciting. And strangely scary, which was a hard thing for a decorated Green Beret Captain to admit to himself. He wasn't supposed to be scared of anything. At least anything that breathes. But this was beyond him. Beyond his training. Way beyond anything he knew.

But Sara, as usual, was way ahead of him and everyone else. And if she was afraid of anything, she sure kept it a secret. When Sam came inside and walked the corridors back to Sara's room, he found a party of happy people laughing and swapping stories about how relieved they were when they heard the news, about how they felt when they saw Jesus and about every other possible personal reflection on what had been the most dramatic and exhilarating series of events that had ever happened in their town. But where was Sara?

Bonnie and Alex looked around. No Sara. Did she slip out somehow? Where to? And why? Panicked, they ran through the halls calling her name until they came to the front lobby where another crowd had gathered. Through the open doors the crowd were watching and quietly listening along with a large gathering outside of news media and general public around the building's front steps – listening to little Sara, who stood outside the doorway and spoke, looking for all the world like a celebrity holding court, or, alright, like a pint-sized preacher.

"Sara!" Bonnie called out.

"I'll be right with you, Mom. I just need to help these people a little."

That line got a laugh from the crowd, to Sara's bemusement. "What was so funny about it?" she thought. But she carried on, in her calm, matter-of-fact way.

"Everybody is asking about 'the Miracle,' like seeing Jesus is something out of this world. Why is that?"

"Because it is out of this world," said one reporter.

"Shouldn't be," said Sara.

"It doesn't happen everyday," said another reporter.

"Oh, but it does. Jesus is here every day. He is everywhere. He is in everyone. He told us that." Then Sara turned to Pastor Jenkins: "Didn't he, Pastor?"

The Pastor, standing off to the side, was momentarily flustered, "Well, yes."

"What does he tell us?...'Whatever you do to the least of these —"

"Yes, yes, 'Whatever you do to the least of these, my brethren, you have done it to me,'" said the Pastor, nodding and smiling approvingly at his young congregant.

"So we're supposed to see him in everyone," Sara went on, "so why does everyone think it's such a big deal when it happens?"

"But what about all the healings, Sara?" asked a reporter.

"I think God can do anything. Sometimes you just have to ask and have faith. And then get out of the way and let him work." Then Sara smiled. "Thank you all for coming out, but I need to go home now. I'm tired."

And as she turned away to re-enter the hospital building and her family closed around her, the crowd of reporters erupted with a roar of questions — about the healings, about her back-from-the-dead experience, about her plans, and so on, and so on, and so on — all the things that media reporters think the public would want to know about a little girl who has caused people to be healed and who has apparently cheated death in every form and has been carried to heaven and back in the arms of Jesus.

Sure, that was powerful stuff. Even Sam and his family couldn't blame the people for all the attention, but they were determined not to let it crush little Sara. They wanted her to keep her innocence and be a little girl from White Dove, not a creature of the media.

Bonnie and Alex came out the front of the building, guiding Danny and Sara by the hand, the kids dressed in blue hoodies to shield them, while the way through the pressing crowd of media and public was cleared by some hospital staff, as well as by Fathers Echevarria and Moretti, along with Chuck Carter and his sons, Nick and Ryan, putting their sizable heft to good use. The Hopkins Family finally got into their blue Ford Explorer and slowly managed to move the vehicle through the crowd and off the parking lot. A caravan of press cars followed them out into the street.

Meanwhile, out the rear door into the back lot came Sam with Maria, Theresa and Theresa's little boy friend, Jack, in a Dodgers cap and a Dodger jacket with "Puig 66" on the back. They all climbed into the truck and drove off, unnoticed.

As they rode through town, Maria said, "You know, I think you should think about coming to church with us."

"I could do that," said Sam, "if you'll come to Pastor Jenkins's church with me now and then. I think my family might want me to be there every once in a while."

Maria looked at him for a moment, then nodded. "Okay. We could do that."

"Then it's a date!" chimed in Theresa.

"Theresa!" Maria exclaimed, blushing at her daughter's forwardness.

"No, that's okay," said Sam, laughing. "That's okay, Theresa. That's good. It is a date. For sure. I'll come by for you, but you'll have to coach me on when to stand up and sit down and kneel and all that. Last time I was in a Catholic church I got pretty confused."

Maria laughed. "You know, I get confused, too, sometimes, but I don't think God really cares."

Maria and Theresa got out at their house in town and Sam and little Jack continued on to the Rancho de la Paloma Blanca, where Jack removed his hat and put on some other clothes that Sam had brought along – clothes more appropriate for the tow-headed little girl that "Jack" actually was.

"Grandpa, we fooled them!" giggled Sara.

"Now, when you see Sylvia Miller," said Sam, "make sure you thank her for being you."

"I will! That was fun!"

"Good. You'll be safe here. I'll put guards at the gates if I have to."

"Thank you, Grandpa. But you know, I am going to want to talk to everybody sooner or later. I don't think Jesus wants me to not talk about him."

Grandpa couldn't stop smiling at his sweet girl. "I know that, Darlin'. But this way, you do it when you're ready. Not just because CNN is at the door."

"Okay," said Sara.

This advice wasn't news to Sara. She was pretty much used to doing everything when she was ready. That had always been her routine. She would pray on a thing and when she felt she had an answer, she didn't question it, she just went ahead and never looked back. So the days to come held no fears for her. She had already died once and it wasn't so bad. What else could they do to her?

And she remembered something that back at the hospital, Father Echevarria had said to her before they left. As the priests began to leave her room, everyone else had already gone for the moment, and Father Echevarria stopped. Father Moretti followed his lead. Father Echevarria turned and came back and said, "Sara, as you were going through all this, were you ever afraid?"

"Yes."

"Were you afraid to die?"

"Oh, no. The dying part was easy. I knew I was with Jesus."

"Then what were you afraid of?"

"Only of hurting Mom and Dad. If I died."

Father Echevarria smiled at her.

Father Moretti asked, "A lot of people doubted you but you didn't let them change you, did you?"

"I never thought of it that way," she replied. "I've always seen things in a way that most other people don't. I always knew that. But I also know that everyone else has their own way of seeing things. Why shouldn't they?"

"Even seeing Jesus?" asked Father Moretti.

"Oh, sure," Sara said, "I think Jesus comes to everyone. But we have to see him in our own way, don't we? How else can we do it?"

Father Echevarria stopped in his mental tracks. And slowly, his smile grew even broader.

Sara smiled back at him. "I guess some people are just better at recognizing him."

EPILOGUE

Sam kept his promise to go to with Maria to her Catholic church and she went with him and his family to Pastor Jenkins' church as well. The families all got together more frequently after Sam and Maria got married – in both churches. Sam never forgot the lesson that little Sara taught him about the power of faith and, being the kind of guy he was, he kept it well for the rest of his days.

And the day that Fathers Alanzo Echevarria and Bernardo Moretti boarded their plane back to Mexico City was the day that, before the flight was over, they both learned in truth how completely Sara Hopkins had changed their lives.

The flight began uneventfully. Their Boeing 737 was filled to capacity and took off to the West over the ocean from LAX. As it gained altitude, they could see in the distance the mountains to the North that cradled the village of White Dove.

As he looked out the starboard window, Father Alanzo said, "I don't think I'll ever get her out of my head."

"You mean Sara?"

Father Alanzo nodded and smiled fondly. "She answered for me the question I had asked every night since I was a child. It came so easy to her." He shook his head and laughed.

"I guess God does have a sense of humor, doesn't he?" said Bernardo.

"You know," said Alanzo, "I don't have that dream anymore."

"About the Statue of Limpias?"

"Not since that day with Sara."

"So you learned the 'Secret of the Miracle?'"

Alanzo found himself nearly giddy at the thought. He nodded and answered, sheepishly. "I believe I did."

Bernardo nodded and smiled. "I think we both learned some secrets from her."

Then, as Bernardo, in the near-sleep reverie that air flights can induce, stared absent-mindedly out the window, he found himself looking at a flame coming out of the starboard engine. Not the nearly invisible blue one that was supposed to come out the tail pipe and drive the aircraft, but a bright orange tongue that flickered through the vents at the top of the wing. And he grew aware that a buzz was going through the cabin as other passengers began seeing the same thing.

Father Alanzo seemed unaware of any of this. He lay back with eyes closed and thought, "It was in front of me the whole time." 'Trust in the visions of the faithful, even as you trust in your faith. Your faith in me.' All of us are different. Each sees God differently. And we all receive God's love and the hope that it creates, each in our own way. Perhaps the real wonder is that more of us don't see that. Praise be to God for the blessing of those who do."

Now an explosion ripped through the flaming engine and blew off half the starboard wing of the aircraft, putting the plane into an uncontrollable horizontal spin, floating downward toward the ocean like a boomerang or a spinning stone.

The cabin was filled with the chaos of hurling laptops and luggage and glasses and bottles and blood amid the screams of the agony of people who saw now their own deaths approaching.

And, yes, Alanzo, too, was by now very wide-awake and exquisitely aware of the ocean of fear the cabin was awash in and the very good reasons for it.

Could they survive the crash into the water that awaited them at the end of their long, spinning, five-minute descent? They both knew the answer was probably not. But Alanzo, like Bernardo, remained placid in the face of the threat. And as they lay strapped into their seats and they looked at each other, they both realized that they were at that moment witnesses and participants in yet another miracle: alone among the passengers, they had no fear and were at peace in the eye of that hurricane, regardless of where and how it may take them. And without having to speak, they both thanked God, each in his own heart, for having met Sara Hopkins and having received through her this greatest of blessings.

THE END

Postscript

In case you may be wondering what finally happened to my granddaughter, whom I mentioned in the Preface, as you may have guessed, our prayers were answered. She survived and did it in a most unexpected way. No, she did not see Jesus, or if she did, she said nothing about it. But looking back on it, I have to feel He was present. Before they took her into surgery, prepping for a very high-risk procedure, I found myself promising God that if she lived, I would create something that would bring a message of faith to the world. What the doctors found when they went in was that her body had spontaneously encased the tumor and they were able to remove it safely and entirely. And she never needed radiation therapy. Her doctors were dumbfounded. They had no medical explanation. Other than a miracle. That was what the doctors thought. And who am I to disagree?

-- G. M. Mercier

Learn more about "The Mustard Seed" and connect with your Christian Community to share your miracles, hear about other Christian miracles and tell your fellow Christians how you found the love of Jesus Christ.

To do this visit us at http://www.themustardseedbook.com

TRAILMAKER PRODUCTIONS, LLC
1310 Venice Blvd., Suite 200
Venice, CA 90291
www.TrailmakerProductions.com
info@themustardseedbook.com